THE PICNIC.　See page 133.

ROLLO'S TOUR
IN
EUROPE.

W. J. REYNOLDS & CO.
Publishers. Boston.

ROLLO IN SCOTLAND,

BY

JACOB ABBOTT.

BOSTON:

W. J. REYNOLDS & COMPANY,

No. 24 CORNHILL.

1856.

STEREOTYPED AT THE
BOSTON STEREOTYPE FOUNDRY.

GEO. C. RAND AND AVERY, PRINTERS, CORNHILL.

CONTENTS.

ENGRAVINGS.

ROLLO'S TOUR IN EUROPE.

ORDER OF THE VOLUMES.

☞ The demand for the above volumes having been large, the author has been induced to write additional volumes, in continuation of this series, which are now in preparation.

STIRLING CASTLE.

ROLLO IN SCOTLAND.

CHAPTER I.

THE BOY THAT WAS NOT LOADED.

One of the ways to Scotland.	Waldron Kennedy.

IN the course of his travels in Europe, Rollo went with his uncle George one summer to spend a fortnight in Scotland.

There are several ways of going into Scotland from England. One way is to take a steamer from Liverpool, and go up the Clyde to Glasgow. This was the route that Mr. George and Rollo took.

On the way from Liverpool to Glasgow, Rollo became acquainted with a boy named Waldron Kennedy. Waldron was travelling with his father and mother and two sisters. His sisters were mild and gentle girls, and always kept near their mother; but Waldron seemed to be always getting into difficulty, or mischief. He was just about Rollo's age, but was a little taller. He was a very strong boy, and full of life and spirits.

He was very venturesome, too, and he was continually frightening his mother by getting himself into, what seemed to her dangerous situa-
tions. One morning, when she came up on deck,
just after the steamer entered the mouth of the
Clyde, she almost fainted away at seeing Waldron half way up the shrouds. He was poising
himself there on one of the ratlines, resting upon
one foot, and holding on with only one hand.

To prevent his doing such things, Waldron's
mother kept him under the closest possible re-
straint, and would hardly let him go away from
her side. She watched him, too, very closely all the
time, and worried him with perpetual cautions.
It was always, "Waldron, don't do this," or,
"Waldron, you must not do that," or, "Waldron,
don't go there." This confinement made Waldron very restless and uneasy; so that, on the
whole, both he himself and his mother, too, had a
very uncomfortable time of it.

"He worries my life out of me," she used to
say, "and spoils all the pleasure of my tour. O,
if he were only a girl!"

Mr. George had been acquainted with Mr.
Kennedy and his family in New York, and they
were all very glad to meet him on board the
steamer.

On the morning after the steamer entered the

mouth of the Clyde, Mrs. Kennedy and her daughters were sitting on a settee upon the deck, with books in their hands. From time to time they read in these books, and in the intervals they looked at the scenery. Waldron stood near them, leaning in a listless manner on the railing. Rollo came up to the place, and accosted Waldron, saying, —

"Come, Waldron, come with me."

"Hush!" said Waldron, in a whisper. "You go out there by the paddle box and wait a moment, till my mother begins to look on her book again, and then I'll steal away and come."

But Rollo never liked to obtain any thing by tricks and treachery, and so he turned to Mrs. Kennedy, and, in a frank and manly manner, said, —

"Mrs. Kennedy, may Waldron go away with me a little while?"

"Why, I am afraid, Rollo," said Mrs. Kennedy. "He always gets into some mischief or other the moment he is out of my sight."

"O, we shall be under my uncle George's care," said Rollo. "I am going out there where he is sitting."

"Well," said Mrs. Kennedy, hesitating, and looking very timid, — "well, Waldron may go a little while. But, Waldron, you must be sure and stay by Mr. George, or, at least, not go any where without his leave."

"Yes," said Waldron, "I will."

So he and Rollo went away, and walked leisurely towards the place where Mr. George was sitting.

"I am glad we are coming up this river, to Greenock and Glasgow," said Waldron.

"Why?" asked Rollo.

"Because of the steamboats," said Waldron.

"Do they build a great many steamboats in Greenock and Glasgow?" asked Rollo.

"Yes," said Waldron; "this is the greatest place for building steamboats in the world."

"Except New York," said Rollo.

"O, of course, except New York," replied Waldron. "But they build all the big English steamers in this river. All the Cunarders were built here, and they have got some of the best machine shops and founderies here that there are in the world. I should like to go all about and see them, if I could only get away from my mother."

"Why, won't she let you go?" said Rollo.

"No," replied Waldron, "not if she knows it. She thinks I am a little boy, and is so afraid that I shall get *hurt!*"

Waldron pronounced the word *hurt* in a

drawling and contemptuous tone, which was so comical that Rollo could not help laughing outright.

"I go to all the ship yards and founderies in New York whenever I please," continued Waldron. "I go when she does not know it. Sometimes the men let me help them carry out the melted iron, and pour it into the moulds."

By this time the two boys had reached the place where Mr. George was. He was sitting on what is called a camp stool, and was engaged in reading his guide book, and studying the map, with a view of finding out what route it would be best to take in the tour they were about making in Scotland. Mr. George drew the boys into conversation with him on the subject. His object was to become acquainted with Waldron, and find out what sort of a boy he was.

"Where do you wish to go, Waldron?" said Mr. George.

"Why, I want to stay here a good many days," said Waldron, "to see the steamers and the dockyards. They are building a monstrous iron ship, somewhere here. She is going to be five hundred tons bigger than the Baltic."

"I should like to see her," said Mr. George.

As he said this he kept his eye upon his map, following his finger, as he moved it about from place to place, as if he was studying out a good way to go.

"There is Edinburgh," said Mr. George; "we must certainly go to Edinburgh."

"Yes," said Waldron, "I suppose that is a pretty great place. Besides, I want to see the houses twelve stories high."

"And there is Linlithgow," continued Mr. George, still looking upon his map. "That is the place where Mary, Queen of Scots, was born. Waldron, would you like to go there?"

"Why, no," said Waldron, doubtfully, "not much. I don't care much about that."

"It is a famous old ruin," said Mr. George.

"But I don't care much about the old ruins," said Waldron. "If the lords and noblemen are as rich as people say they are, I should think they would mend them up."

"And here, off in the western part of Scotland," continued Mr. George, "are a great many mountains. Would you like to go and see the mountains?"

"No, sir," said Waldron, "not particularly." Then in a moment he added, "Can we go up to the top of them, Mr. George?"

"Yes," said Mr. George, "we can go to the top of some of them."

"The highest?" asked Waldron.

"Yes," said Mr. George. "Ben Nevis, I be-lieve, is the highest. We can go to the top of that."

"Then I should like to go," said Waldron, eagerly.

"Unless," continued Mr. George, "it should rain *too* hard."

"O, I should not care for the rain," said Wal-dron. "It's good fun to go in the rain."

While this conversation had been going on, Waldron had been looking this way and that, at the various ships and steamers that were gliding about on the water, examining carefully the building of each one, and watching her mo-tions. He now proposed that Rollo should go forward to the bridge with him, where they could have a better lookout.

"Well," said Rollo. So the two boys went together to the bridge.

The bridge was a sort of narrow platform, extending across the steamer, from one paddle wheel to the other, for the captain or pilot to walk upon, in order to see how the steamer was going, and to direct the steering. When they are in the open sea any of the passengers are allowed to walk here; but in coming into port, or into a river crowded with shipping, then a notice is put up requesting passengers not to go

2

upon the bridge, inasmuch as at such times it is required for the exclusive use of the captain and pilot.

This notice was up when Waldron and Rollo reached the bridge.

" See," said Rollo, pointing at the notice. " We cannot go there."

" O, never mind that," said Waldron. " They'll let us go. They only mean that they don't want too many there — that's all."

But Rollo would not go. Mr. George had accustomed him, in travelling about the world, always to obey all lawful rules and orders, and particularly every direction of this kind which he might find in public places. Some people are very much inclined to crowd upon the line of such rules, and even to encroach upon them till they actually encounter some resistance to drive them back. They do this partly to show their independence and importance. But Mr. George was not one of this sort.

So Rollo would not go upon the bridge.

" Then let us go out on the forecastle," said Waldron. He pointed, as he spoke, to the forecastle, which is a small raised deck at the bows of a steamer, where there is an excellent place to see.

" No," said Rollo, " I will not go on the fore-

castle either. Uncle George's rule for me on
board ship is, that I may go where I see other
gentlemanly passengers go, and nowhere else.
The passengers do not go on the forecastle."

"Yes," said Waldron, "there are some there
now."

"There is only one," said Rollo, "and he has
no business there."

During the progress of this conversation the
boys had sat down upon the upper step of a steep
flight of stairs which led down from the promenade
deck to the main deck. They could see pretty
well where they were, but not so well, Waldron
thought, as they could have seen from the forecastle.

"*I* think we might go on the forecastle as well
as not," said Waldron, "even according to your
own rule. For there is a passenger there."

"I think it is doubtful," said Rollo.

"Well," said Waldron, "we'll call it doubtful.
We will draw lots for it."

So saying, Waldron put his hand in his pocket,
and, after fumbling about there a minute or two,
took it out, and held it before Rollo with the fin-
gers shut, so that Rollo could not see what was
in it.

"Odd or even?" said Waldron.

Rollo looked at the closed hand, with a smile of curiosity on his face, but he did not answer.

"Say odd or even," continued Waldron. "If you hit, that will prove that you are right, and we will not go to the forecastle; but if you miss, then we *will* go."

Rollo hesitated a moment, not being quite sure that this was a proper way of deciding a question of right and wrong. In a moment, however, he answered, "Even."

Waldron opened his hand, and Rollo saw that there was *nothing* in it.

"There," said Waldron, "it is odd, and you said even."

"No," said Rollo, "it is not either even *or* odd. There is nothing at all in your hand."

"Well," said Waldron, "nothing is a number, and it is odd."

"O Waldron!" said Rollo, "it is not any number at all. Besides, if it is a number, it is not odd — it is even."

"Yes," said Waldron, "it is a number, for you can add it, and subtract it, and multiply it, and divide it, just as you can any other number."

"O Waldron!" exclaimed Rollo again. "You can't do any such thing."

"Yes," said Waldron, "I can add nothing to

ODD OR EVEN.

one, and it makes one. So, I can take nothing away from one, and it leaves one.

"I can multiply nothing, too. I can multiply it by ten. Ten times nothing are nothing. So I can divide it. Five in nothing no times, and nothing over."

Rollo was somewhat perplexed by this argument, and he did not know what to reply. Still he would not admit that nothing was a number — still less that it was an odd number. He did not believe, he said, that it was any number at all. The boys continued the discussion * for some time, and then they concluded to go and refer it to Mr. George.

And here I ought to say that Waldron had an artful design in taking nothing in his hand, when he called upon Rollo to say, Odd or even. He did it in order that whatever answer Rollo might give, he might attempt to prove it wrong. He was a very ingenious boy, and could as easily maintain that nothing was even as that it was odd. Whichever Rollo had said, his plan was to maintain the contrary, and so persuade him to go to the forecastle.

Mr. George was very much pleased when the

---

* The conversation was a discussion, and not a dispute, for it was calm, quiet, and good-tempered throughout. A dispute is an *angry* discussion.

boys brought the question to him. Indeed, almost all people are pleased when boys come to
them in an amicable manner, to have their con-
troversies settled. Then, besides, he inferred
from the nature of the question that had arisen
in this case, that Waldron was a boy of considerable thinking powers, or else he would not
have taken any interest in a purely intellectual
question like this.

"Well," said Mr. George, "that is quite a
curious question. But before I decide it you
must first both of you give me your reasons.
What makes you think nothing is an odd number, Waldron?"

"I don't know," said Waldron, hesitating.
"I think it looks kind of odd."

Mr. George smiled at this reason, and then
asked Rollo what made him think it was an
even number.

"I don't think it is an even number," said
Rollo. "I don't think it is any number at all.

"However," continued Rollo, "that is not the
real question, after all. The real question is,
whether we shall go on the forecastle or not, to
have a lookout."

"No," said Mr. George, "it is not according
to etiquette at sea for the passengers to go on
the forecastle."

" But they do," said Waldron.

" Yes," said Mr. George, " they sometimes do, I know ; and sometimes, under peculiar circumstances, it is right for them to go ; but as a general rule, it is not. That is the place for the sailors to occupy in working the ship. It is something like the kitchen in a hotel. What should you think of the guests at a hotel, if they went down into the kitchen to see what was going on there ? "

Rollo laughed aloud.

" But we don't go to the forecastle to see what is going on there," said Waldron ; " we go for a lookout — to see what is going on away ahead, on the water."

" True," said Mr. George, " and that is a very important difference, I acknowledge. I don't think my comparison holds good."

Mr. George was always very candid in all his arguing. It is of very great importance that all persons should be so, especially when reasoning with boys. It teaches *them* to be candid.

Just at this time Waldron's attention was attracted by the appearance of a very large steamer, which now came suddenly into view, with its great red funnel pouring out immense volumes of black smoke. Waldron ran over to the other side of the deck to see it. Rollo followed, and thus the explanation which Mr. George might have given, in respect to the arithmetical nature and relations of nothing were necessarily postponed to some future time.

About half an hour after this, while Rollo was sitting by the side of his uncle, looking at the map, and trying to find out how soon they should come in sight of the famous old Castle of Dunbarton, which stands on a rocky hill upon the banks of the Clyde, Mr. Kennedy came up to him to inquire if he knew where Waldron was.

Rollo said that he did not know. He had not seen him for some time.

"We can't find him any where," said Mr. Kennedy. "We have looked all over the ship. His mother is half crazy. She thinks he has fallen overboard."

So Rollo and Mr. George both rose immediately and went off to see if they could find Waldron. They went in various directions, inquiring of every body they met if they had seen such a boy. Several people had seen him half an hour before, when he was with Rollo ; but no one knew where he had been since. At last, in about ten minutes, Rollo came running to Mrs. Kennedy, who was walking about through the cabins in great distress, and said, hurriedly, "I've found

him; he is safe," and then ran off to tell Mr.
Kennedy.

Mrs. Kennedy followed him, calling out eagerly,
"Where is he? Where is he?" Rollo met Mr.
Kennedy at the head of the cabin stairs, and he
seemed very much rejoiced to learn that Waldron was found. Rollo led the way, and Mr.
and Mrs. Kennedy followed him, until they came
to a place on the deck, pretty well forward,
where there was an opening surrounded by an
iron railing, through which you could look down
into the hold below. It was very far down that
you could look, and at different distances on the
way were to be seen iron ladders going from
deck to deck, and ponderous shafts, moving continually, with great clangor and din, while at the
bottom were seen the mouths of several great
glowing furnaces, with men at work shovelling
coal into them.

" There he is," said Rollo, pointing down.

Mr. and Mrs. Kennedy leaned over the railing
and looked down, and there they beheld Waldron, hard at work shovelling coal into the mouth
of a furnace, with a shovel which he had bor-
rowed of one of the men. In a word, Waldron
had turned stoker.

Mr. Kennedy hurried down the ladders to

bring Waldron up, while Mr. George and Rollo went back to the deck.

About an hour after this Mr. Kennedy came and took a seat on a settee where Mr. George was sitting, and began to talk about Waldron.

"He is the greatest plague of my life," said Mr. Kennedy. "I don't know what I shall do with him. He is continually getting into some mischief. I have shut him up a close prisoner in the state room, and I am going to keep him there till we land. But it will do no good. It will not be an hour after he gets out before he will be in some new scrape. You know a great deal about boys; I wish you would tell me what to do with him."

"I think, if he was under my charge," said Mr. George, very quietly, "I should *load* him."

"Load him?" repeated Mr. Kennedy, inquiringly.

"Yes," said Mr. George, "I mean I should give him a load to carry."

"I don't understand, exactly," said Mr. Kennedy. "What is your idea?"

"My idea is," said Mr. George, "that a growing boy, especially if he is a boy of unusual capacity, is like a steam engine in this respect. A steam engine must always have a load to carry, — that is, something to *employ* and *absorb* the force it is capable of exerting, — or else it will break itself to pieces with it. The force *will* expend itself on something, and if you don't load it with something good, it will employ itself in mischief.

"Here now is the engine of this ship," continued Mr. George. "Its force is conducted to the paddle wheels, where it has full employment for itself in turning the wheels against the immense resistance of the water, and in carrying the ship along. This work is its *load*. If this load were to be taken off, — for example, if the steamer were to be lifted up out of the water so that the wheels could spin round in the air, — the engine would immediately stave itself to pieces, for want of having any thing else to expend its energies upon."

"Yes," said Mr. Kennedy. "I have no doubt of it."

"Now, I think," continued Mr. George, "that it is in some sense the same with a boy whose mental and physical powers are in good condition. These powers must be employed. They hunger and thirst for employment, and if they don't get it in doing good they will be sure to find it in some kind of mischief."

"Well," said Mr. Kennedy, with a sigh, "there

is a great deal in that; but what is to be done?
You can't *employ* such a boy as that. There is
nothing he can do. I wish you would take him,
and see if you can load him, as you call it. Take
him with you on this tour you are going to make
in Scotland. I will put money in your hands to
cover his expenses, and you may charge any
thing you please beyond, for your care of him."

"Perhaps his mother would not like such an
arrangement," said Mr. George.

"O, yes," replied Mr. Kennedy; "nothing
would please her more."

"And would Waldron like it himself?" asked
Mr. George.

"I presume so," said Mr. Kennedy; "he likes
any thing that is a change."

Mr. Kennedy went down to the state room
to see Waldron, and ask him what he thought
of this plan. Waldron said he should like it
very much. So he was at once liberated from
his confinement, and transferred to Mr. George's
charge.

"Now, Waldron," said Mr. George, when
Waldron came to him, "I shall want some help
from you about getting ashore from the boat. Do
you think you could go ashore with Rollo as
soon as we land, and take a cab and go directly
up to the hotel, and engage rooms for us, while I

am looking out for the baggage, and getting it ready ? "

" Yes, sir ; yes, sir," said Waldron, eagerly. " I can do that.   What hotel shall I go to ? "

" I don't know," said Mr. George.   " I don't know any thing about the hotels in Glasgow. You must find out."

" Well," said Waldron, "only how shall I find out ? "

" I am sure *I* don't know," said Mr. George. " I leave it all to you and Rollo.   I am busy forming my plans for a tour.   You and Rollo can go and talk about it, and see if you can discover any way of finding out the name of one of the best hotels.   If you can't, after trying fifteen minutes, come to me, and I will help you."

So saying, Mr. George began to study his map again, and Waldron, apparently much pleased with his commission, said, " Come, Rollo," and walked away.

CHAPTER II.

DISTRICTS OF SCOTLAND.

I THINK that Mr. George was quite right in his idea, that the true remedy for the spirit of restlessness and mischief that Waldron manifested was to employ him, or, as he metaphorically termed it, to *load* him. And as this volume will, perhaps, fall into the hands of many parents as well as children, I will here remark that a great many good-hearted and excellent boys fall into the same difficulty from precisely the same cause ; namely, that they have not adequate employment for their mental and physical powers, which are growing and strengthening every day, and are hungering and thirsting for the means and opportunities of expending their energies.

Parents are seldom aware how fast their children are growing and increasing in strength, both of body and mind. The evidences of this growth, in respect to the limbs and muscles of the body, are, indeed, obvious to the eye ; and as the growth advances, we have continual proof of the pleasure which the exercise of these new powers gives to the possessor of them. The active and boisterous plays of boys derive their chief charm from the pleasure they feel in testing and exercising their muscular powers in every way. They are always running, and leaping, and wrestling, and pursuing each other, and pushing each other, and climbing up to high places, and standing on their heads, and walking on the tops of fences, and performing all other possible or conceivable feats, which may give them the pleasure of working, in new and untried ways, their muscular machinery, and feeling its increasing power, and in producing new effects by means of it. They get themselves into continual difficulties and dangers by these things, and cause themselves a great deal of suffering. Still they go on, for the intoxicating delight of using their powers, or, rather, the irresistible instinct which impels them to use them, has greater force with them than all other considerations.

We see all this very plainly in respect to the action of the limbs and organs of the body ; for it is palpably evident to our senses, and we feel the necessity of providing safe and proper modes of expending these energies. Since we find, for example, that boys must kick something, we give them a football to kick ; which, being a mere

3

ball of wind, may be kicked without doing any
harm. And so with almost all the other play-
things and sports which are devised for boys, or
which they devise for themselves. They are the
means, simply, of enabling them to employ their
growing powers and expand their energies, without doing any body any harm. We know very
well that it is not safe to leave these powers and
energies unemployed.

But we are very apt to forget that there are
powers and faculties of the mind, equally vigor-
ous, and equally eager to be exercised, that ought
also to be provided for. The strength of the
will, the power of exercising judgment and discretion, the spirit of enterprise, the love of command, and other such mental impulses, are growing and strengthening every day, in every healthy
boy, and they are all clamorous for employment.
The instinct that impels them is so strong that
they will find employment in some way or other
for themselves, unless an occupation is otherwise
provided for them. A very large proportion of
the acts of mischievousness and wrong which
boys commit arise from this cause. Even boys
who are bad enough to form a midnight scheme
for robbing an orchard, are influenced mainly in
perpetrating the deed, not by the pleasure of
eating the apples which they expect to obtain by

it, but by the pleasure of forming a scheme, of
contriving ways and means of surmounting difficulties, of watching against surprises, of braving
dangers, of successfully attaining to a desired
end over and through a succession of obstacles
interposing. This view of the case does not show
that such deeds are right; it only shows the
true nature of the wrong involved in them, and
helps us in discovering and applying the remedy.

At least this was Mr. George's view of the
case in respect to Waldron, when he heard how
often he was getting into difficulty by his ad-
venturous and restless character. He thought
that the remedy was, as he expressed it, to *load*
him; that is, to give to the active and enter-
prising spirit of his mind something to expend
his energies upon. It required great tact and
discretion, and great knowledge of the habits
and characteristics of boyhood, to enable him to
do this; but Mr. George possessed these quali-
ties in a high degree.

But to return to the story.

Mr. George had decided on coming into Scotland from Liverpool by water, because that was
the cheapest way of getting into the heart of the
country. And here, in order that you may understand the course of Rollo's travels, I must
pause to explain the leading geographical features

of the country. If you read this explanation
carefully, and follow it on the map, you will understand the subsequent narrative much better
than you otherwise would do.

You will see, then, by looking at any map,
that Scotland is separated from England by two
rivers which flow from the interior of the country
into the sea — one towards the east, and the other
towards the west. The one on the east side is the
Tweed. The Tweed forms the frontier between
England and Scotland for a considerable distance, and is, therefore, often spoken of as the
boundary between the two countries. Indeed,
the phrase " beyond the Tweed " is often used in
England to denote Scotland. In former times,
when England and Scotland were independent
kingdoms, incessant wars were carried on across
this border, and incursions were made by the
chieftains from each realm into the territories of
the other, and castles were built on many com-
manding points to defend the ground. The ruins
of many of these old castles still remain.

On the western side of the island the boundary
between England and Scotland is formed by a
very wide river, or rather river's mouth, called
Solway Frith. Between this Solway Frith and
the Tweed, the boundary which separates the
two countries runs along the summit of a range

of hills. This range of hills thus forms a sort of neck of high land, which prevents the Tweed and the Solway Frith from* cutting Scotland off from England altogether, and making a separate island of it.

About seventy or eighty miles to the northward of the boundary the land is almost cut in two again by two other rivers, with broad mouths, which rise pretty near together in the interior of the country, and flow — one to the east and the other to the west — into the two seas.

These rivers are the Forth and the Clyde. The Forth flows to the east, and has a very wide estuary,* as you will see by the map. The Clyde, on the other hand, flows to the west. Its estuary is long and crooked.

The Forth and the Clyde, with their estuaries, almost cut Scotland in two ; and by means of them ships and steamers from all parts of England and from foreign ports are enabled to come into the very heart of the country.

The two largest and most celebrated cities in Scotland are situated in the valleys of these rivers, the Forth and the Clyde. They are

---

* An estuary is a sort of bay, produced by the widening of a river at its mouth. Scotland is remarkable for the estuaries which are formed at the mouths of its rivers. They are called there *friths*.

Edinburgh and Glasgow. Edinburgh is on the
Forth, though situated at some little distance
from its banks. Glasgow is on the Clyde. There
is a railway extending across from Edinburgh to
Glasgow, and also a canal, connecting the waters
of the Forth with the Clyde. The region of
these cities, and of the canal and railroad which
connects them, is altogether the busiest, the most
densely peopled, and the most important portion
of Scotland; and this is the reason why Mr.
George wished to come directly into it by water
from Liverpool.

The cities of Glasgow and Edinburgh, though
both greatly celebrated, are celebrated in very
different ways. Edinburgh is the city of science,
of literature, and of the arts. Here are many
learned institutions, the fame and influence of
which extend to every part of the world. Here
are great book publishing establishments, which
send forth millions of volumes every year —
from ponderous encyclopædias of science, and
elegantly illustrated and costly works of art,
down to tracts for Sabbath schools, and picture
books for children. The situation of Edinburgh
is very romantic and beautiful; the town being
built among hills and ravines of the most picturesque and striking character. When Scotland
was an independent kingdom Edinburgh was the

capital of it, and thus the old palace of the kings and the royal castle are there, and the town has been the scene of some of the most remarkable events in the Scottish history.

Glasgow, on the other hand, which is on the Clyde, towards the western side of the island, together with all the country for many miles around it, forms the scene of the mechanical and manufacturing industry of Scotland. The whole district, in fact, is one vast workshop; being full of mines, mills, forges, furnaces, machine shops, ship yards and iron works, with pipes every where puffing out steam, and tall chimneys, higher, some of them, than the Bunker Hill Monument, or the steeple of Trinity Church, in New York. These tall chimneys are seen rising every where, all around the horizon, and sending up volumes of dense black smoke, which comes pouring incessantly from their summits, and thence floating majestically away, mingles itself with the clouds of the sky.

The reason of this is, that the strata of rocks which lie beneath the ground in all this region consist, in a great measure, of beds of coal and of iron ore. The miners dig down in almost any spot, and find iron ore; and very near it, and sometimes in the same pit, they find plenty of coal. These pits are like monstrous wells; very

wide at the mouth, and extending down four or
five times as far as the height of the tallest
steeples, into the bowels of the earth. Over the
mouth of the pit the workmen build a machine,
with ropes and a monstrous wheel, to hoist the
coal and iron up by, and all around they set up
furnaces to smelt the ore and turn it into iron.
Then, at suitable places in various parts of the
country, they construct great rolling mills and
founderies. The rolling mills are to turn the
pig iron into wrought iron, and to manufacture
it into bars and sheets, and rails for the railroads ; and the founderies are to cast it into the
form of great wheels, and cylinders, and beams
for machinery, or for any other purpose that may
be required.

The mines in the valley of the Clyde were
worked first chiefly for the coal, and the coal was
used to drive steam machinery for spinning and
weaving, and for other manufacturing purposes.
The river was in those days a small and insignifi-
cant stream. It was only about five feet deep, so
that the vessels that came to take away the coal
and the manufactured goods had to stop near the
mouth of it, and the cargoes were brought down
to them in boats and lighters. But in process of
time they widened and deepened the river. They
dug out the mud from the bottom of it, and built

walls along the banks ; and in the course of the last hundred years, they have improved it so much that now the largest ships can come quite up to Glasgow. The water is eighteen or twenty feet deep all the way.

The Clyde is the river on which steamboats were first built in Great Britain. The man who was the first in England or Scotland that found a way of making a steam engine that could be put in a boat and made to turn paddle wheels so as to drive the boat along, was James Watt, who was born on the Clyde ; and he is accordingly considered as the author and originator of English steam navigation, just as Fulton is regarded as the originator of the art in America. The Clyde, of course, very naturally became the centre of steamboat and steamship building. The iron for the engines was found close at hand, as well as abundant supplies of coal for the fires. The timber they brought from the Baltic. At length, however, they found that they could build ships of iron instead of wood, using iron beams for the framing, and covering them with plates of iron riveted together instead of planks. These ships were found very superior, in almost all respects, to those built of timber ; and as iron in great abundance was found all along the banks of the Clyde, and as the workmen in the region

were extremely skilful in working it, the business of building ships and steamers of this ma-
terial increased wonderfully, until, at length, the
banks of the river for miles below Glasgow became lined with ship yards, where countless
steamers, of monstrous length and graceful forms,
in all the stages of construction, lie ; now sloping
towards the water and down the stream, ready at
the appointed time to glide majestically into the
river, and thence to plough their way to every
portion of the habitable globe.

It was into this busy scene of mechanical industry and skill that our party of travellers were
now coming. But before I resume the narrative
of their adventures, I will say a word about
those parts of Scotland which lie to the north
and south of these central regions that are occupied by the valleys of the Forth and the Clyde.
The region which extends to the southward — that
is, which lies between the valleys of the Forth
and the Clyde on the one hand, and the English
frontier on the other — is called the southern part
of the country. It consists, generally, of fertile
and gently undulating land, which is employed
almost entirely for tillage, and is but little visited by tourists or travellers.

The northern part of Scotland is, however, of
a very different character ; being wild, mountain-

ous and waste, and filled every where with the
most grand and sublime scenery. The eastern por-.
tion of this part of the island is more level, and
there are several large and flourishing towns on or
near the shores of it, such as Inverness, Aberdeen,
Dundee, Perth, and others. But the whole of the
western side of it consists of one vast congeries
of lakes and mountains, so wild and sombre in
their character that they have become celebrated
throughout the world for the gloomy grandeur
of the scenery which they present to the view.

These are the famous Scottish Highlands. Mr.
George's plan was first to visit the valley of the
Clyde, and its various mines and manufactories,
and then to take a circuit round among the
Highlands, on his way to Edinburgh.

CHAPTER III.

ARRIVAL AT GLASGOW.

ONE of the greatest drawbacks to the pleasure
of travelling in Scotland, especially among the
Highlands, is the rain. It usually rains more in
mountainous countries than in those that are
level, for the mountains, rising into the higher
and colder regions of the atmosphere, chill and
condense the vapors that are floating there, on
the same principle by which a tumbler or a
pitcher, made cold by iced water placed within
it, condenses the moisture from the air, upon the
outside of it, on a summer's day. It is also
probable that the mountain summits produce certain effects in respect to the electrical condition
of the atmosphere, on which it is well known
that the formation of clouds and the falling of
rain greatly depend — though this subject is yet
very little understood. At all events, the western
part of Scotland is one of the most rainy regions
in the world, and travellers who visit it must
expect to have their plans and arrangements very

often and very seriously interfered with by the state of the weather.

The changes are quite unexpected too ; for sometimes you will see dark masses of watery vapor, coming suddenly into view, and driving swiftly across the sky, where a few moments before every thing had appeared settled and serene. These scuds are soon followed by others, more and more dense and threatening, until, at last, there come drenching showers of rain, which drive every body to the nearest shelter, if there is any shelter at hand.

Such a change as this came on while Mr. George had been making arrangements with Mr. Kennedy for taking Waldron under his charge ; and just as Waldron and Rollo had gone away to see what plan they could devise in respect to the hotel, it began to rain. The clouds and mists, too, concealed the shores almost entirely from view, and the passengers began to go below. Mr. George followed their example. On his way he passed a sheltered place where he saw Waldron and Rollo engaged in conversation, and he told them, as he passed them, that when they were ready to report they would find him below.

In about fifteen minutes the boys came down to him.

"Uncle George," said Rollo, "we have found

out that there are a good many excellent hotels
in Glasgow, but we think we had better go to
the Queen's."

"Yes, sir," said Waldron. "It fronts on a
handsome square, where they are going to have
an exhibition of flowers to-morrow, with tents
and music."

"And shall you wish to go and see the flowers?" asked Mr. George.

"No, sir," said Waldron. "I don't care much
about the flowers, but I should like to see the
tents, and to hear the music."

"Then, besides, uncle George," said Rollo, "we
are coming to the mouth of the river pretty soon,
and as soon as we get in we shall come to Greenock; and there is a railroad from Greenock up to
Glasgow, so that we can go ashore there, if you
please, and go up to Glasgow quick by the railroad. A great many of the passengers are going
to do that."

"Do you think that would be a good plan?"
asked Mr. George.

"Why, yes," said Rollo, "I *should* think it
would be a good plan, if we had not paid our
passage through by the steamer."

"And what do *you* think about it, Waldron?"
asked Mr. George.

"I should like it," said Waldron. "The fare

is only one and sixpence. I should have preferred to go up in the steamer if it had been pleasant, so that we could see the ships and steamers
on the stocks ; but it is so misty and rainy that
we cannot see any thing at all. So, if you would
go up by the railroad, and then, to-morrow, when
it is pleasant, come down a little way again, on
one of the steamboats, to see the river, I should
like it very mnch."

"But I shall have to stay at home to-morrow,"
said Mr. George, "and write letters to send to
America. It is the last day."

"Then let Rollo and me go down by ourselves," said Waldron.

"Yes, uncle George," said Rollo, "let us go
by ourselves."

"Ah," said Mr. George. "I am not sure that
that would be safe. I am not much acquainted
with Waldron yet, and I don't know what his
character is, in respect to judgment and discretion."

"O, I think he has got good judgment," said
Rollo. "We will both be very careful."

"Yes, sir," said Waldron, "we certainly will."

"O, boys' promises," said Mr. George, "in
respect to such things as that, are good for
nothing at all. I never place any reliance upon
them whatover."

" O uncle George! " exclaimed Rollo.

" Well, now, would you, if you were in my
case? " said Mr. George. " I will leave it to you,
Waldron. Suppose a strange boy, that you know
no more about than I do of you, were to come to
you with a promise that he would be *very careful*
if you would let him go somewhere, and that he
would not go into any dangerous places, or ex-
pose himself to any risks, — would you think it
safe to trust him? "

" Why, no, sir," said Waldron, reluctantly. " I
don't think I should. Perhaps I might *try* him."

"According to my experience," said Mr. George,
" you can't trust to boys' promises in the least.
It is not that they make promises with the inten-
tion of breaking them, but they don't know what
breaking them is. A boy who is not careful does
not know the difference between being careful
and being careless ; and so he breaks his promise,
and then, if he gets into any trouble by his folly,
he says, 'I did not think there was any harm in
that.'

" No," added Mr. George, in conclusion, shaking
his head gravely as he spoke. " I never place
any reliance on such promises."

" Then how can you tell whether to trust a boy
or not? " asked Rollo.

" I never can tell," said Mr. George, " until he

is proved. When he is tried and proved, then I know him; but not before."

"Well," said Rollo, "then let Waldron and me go down the river to-morrow, if it is pleasant, and let that be for our trial."

"It might, possibly, be a good plan to let you go, on that ground," said Mr. George. He said this in a musing manner, as if considering the question.

"I will think of it," said he. "I'll see if I can think of any conditions on which I can allow you to go, and I will tell you about it at the hotel. And now, in regard to going up to Glasgow. I'll leave it to you and Waldron to decide. You must go and ascertain all the facts — such as how soon the train leaves after we arrive, and how much sooner we shall get up there, if we go in it. Then you must take charge of all the baggage, too, and see that it goes across safe from the steamer to the station, and attend to the whole business."

"Yes, sir," said Waldron, "we will. We'll get a cab, and put the baggage right in."

"Can't you get it across without a cab?" said Mr. George. "I don't see how I can afford to take a cab, very well; for you see we have to incur an extra expense as it is, to go in the cars at

4

all, since we have already paid our passage up by the steamer."

"Well, sir," said Waldron, eagerly, "we can carry the baggage across ourselves. Let us go and look at it, Rollo, and see how much there is."

So the boys went off with great eagerness to look at the baggage. In a few minutes they returned again, wearing very bright and animated countenances.

"Yes, sir," said Waldron, "we can take it all just as well as not. I can take your valise, and Rollo can take my things, and I can carry your knapsack under my arm."

"O, I am willing to help," said Mr. George. "I can help in carrying the things, provided I do not have any *care*. If you will count up all the things that are to go, and see that they all do go, and then count them again when we get into the railway carriage, so as to be sure that they are all there, and thus save me from responsibility, that is all I ask, and I will carry any thing you choose to give me."

"Well, sir," said Waldron.

Indeed, Waldron was very much pleased to find how completely Mr. George was putting the business under his and Rollo's charge.

"And now," said Mr. George, "I think you had better tell your father and mother about this plan of our going ashore at Greenock. They may like to do so, too."

" O, they know all about it," said Waldron, and they are going. Mother says that she has had enough of the steamer."

Not long after this the steamer arrived at Greenock, and made fast to the pier. A large number of the passengers went ashore. The rain had ceased, which was very fortunate for those who were to walk to the station ; though, of course, the streets were still wet. As soon as the boat was made fast, Mr. George went to the plank, and there he found Waldron and Rollo ready, with the baggage in their hands. Mr. George took his valise, though at first Waldron was quite unwilling to give it up.

" O, yes," said Mr. George ; " I have no objection to hard work. What I don't like is care. If you and Rollo will take the care off my mind, that is all I ask."

" Well," said Waldron, " we will. And now I wonder which way we must go, to get to the station."

" I am sure I don't know," said Mr. George. As he said this his countenance assumed a vacant and indifferent expression, as if he considered that the finding of the way to the station was no concern of his.

" Ah ! " exclaimed Waldron, " this is the way.
See ! " So saying, Waldron pointed to a sign
put up near the end of the pier, with the words
RAILROAD STATION painted upon it, and a hand
indicating the way to go.

As the sun had now come out, the party had
quite a pleasant walk to the station. Mr. George
had all his clothes in a light and small valise,
which he could carry very easily in his hand.
Some of Rollo's clothes were in this valise, too,
and the rest were in a small carpet bag. Waldron's were in a carpét bag, too. Besides these
things there were some coats and umbrellas to be
carried in the hand, and Mr. George and Rollo
had each a knapsack, which they had bought in
Switzerland. These knapsacks were hung at
their sides. They were light, for at this time
there was very little in them.

Rollo and Waldron stopped once in the street
to inquire if they were on the right way to the
station ; and finding that they were, they went
on, and soon arrived at the gateway. They went
in at a spacious entrance, and thence ascended a
long and very wide flight of stairs, which led to
the second story. There they found an area, covered with a glass roof, and surrounded with offices
of various kinds pertaining to the station. In
the centre was a train of cars, with a locomotive

at the head of it, apparently all ready for a start. Passengers were walking to and fro on the platform, and getting into the carriages.

On one side was a book stand, where a boy was selling books. There was a counter before, and shelves against the walls behind. The shelves were filled with books. These books were in fancy-colored paper bindings, and seemed to consist chiefly of guide books and tales, and other similar works suited to the wants of travellers.

Mr. George laid his valise down upon a bench near by, and began to look at the books. Waldron and Rollo put their baggage down in the same way, and followed his example.

While they were standing there they saw Mr. and Mrs. Kennedy and the two girls coming up the stairs. They were accompanied by a porter.

Mrs. Kennedy stopped a moment to speak to Waldron as she went by.

"Now, Waldron," said she, "you must be very careful, and not get into any difficulty. Keep close to Mr. George all the time, and don't get run over when you get in and out of the cars. You had better button up your jacket. It is very damp, and you will take cold, I am afraid."

So saying, she began to button up Waldron's

jacket in front, giving it a pull this way and that to make it set better.

"Don't, mother!" said Waldron. "I'm so hot."

So he shook his shoulders a little uneasily, and tried to turn away. But his mother insisted that his jacket should be buttoned up, at least part way.

" Come, my dear," said Mr. Kennedy, speaking to his wife; " we have no time to lose. The train is going."

So Mr. Kennedy bade Waldron good by, and hurried on, and Waldron immediately unbuttoned his jacket again, saying at the same time, —

" Come, Mr. George, it is time for us to go aboard."

" Have you got the tickets?" said Mr. George, quietly, still keeping his eyes upon a book that he was examining.

"No," said Waldron. "Are *we* to get the tickets?"

" Of course," said Mr. George. " I have nothing to do with it. You and Rollo have undertaken to get me to Glasgow without my having any thought or concern about it."

" Well, come, Rollo, quick ; let's go and get them. Where's the booking office?"

At the English stations the place where the tickets are bought is called the booking office.

It is necessary to procure tickets, or you cannot commence the journey ; for it is not customary, as in America, to allow the passengers the privilege, when they desire it, of paying in the cars.

" Do you know where the booking office is, Mr. George ? " said Waldron.

" No," said Mr. George, " but if you look about you will find it."

So Waldron and Rollo ran off to find the office. It was down stairs. Before they came back with the tickets the train was gone.

" It is no matter," said Mr. George. " Indeed, I think it is my fault rather than yours, for it was not distinctly understood that you were to get the tickets. There will be another train pretty soon, I presume. In the mean time I should like to look at these books, and you and Rollo can amuse yourselves about the station."

So Waldron and Rollo went off to see if they could find a time table, in order to learn when the next train would go. They found that there would be another train in an hour. In the mean time it began to rain again, which prevented the party from taking a walk about the town ; so they had to amuse themselves at the station as they best could.

There was a refreshment room at the station, and the boys thought at first that it would be a good plan to have something to eat ; but, finally, they concluded that they would wait, and have a regular dinner at the coffee room of the hotel. Mr. George left them to decide the question themselves as they thought best.

The hour, however, soon glided away, and at the end of it the party took their seats in the train, and were trundled rapidly along the banks of the river to Glasgow. The road lay through beautiful parks a considerable portion of the way, with glimpses of the water here and there between the trees. The view of the scenery, however, was very much impeded by the falling rain.

CHAPTER IV.

THE EXPEDITION PLANNED.

THE boys were very successful in their selection of a hotel, for the Queen's Hotel, in Glasgow, is one of the most comfortable and best managed inns in the kingdom.

The party *rode* to the inn, in a cab which they took at the station in Glasgow, when the train arrived there, instead of walking, as they had done in going from the boat to the station at Greenock. The boys asked Mr. George's advice on this point, and he said that, though he was unwilling to take any responsibility, he had no objection whatever to giving his advice, whenever they wished for it. So he told them that he thought it was always best to go to a hotel in a carriage of some sort.

" Because," said he, " in England and Scotland, — that is, in all the great towns, — if we come on foot, they think that we are poor, and of no consequence, and so give us the worst rooms, and pay us very little attention."

When the cab arrived at the hotel Waldron
said, —

"There, Mr. George, we have brought you
safe to the hotel. Now we have nothing more to
do. We give up the command to you now."

"Very well," said Mr. George.

Two or three nicely dressed porters and wait-
ers came out from the door of the hotel, to receive the travellers and wait upon them in. The
porters took the baggage, even to the coats and
umbrellas, and the head waiter led the way into
the house. Waldron paid the cabman as he
stepped out of the cab. He knew what the fare
was, and he had it all ready. Mr. George said
to the waiter that he wanted two bedrooms,
one with two beds in it. The waiter bowed, with
an air of great deference and respect, and said
that the chambermaid would show the rooms.
The chambermaid, who was a very nice-looking
and tidily-dressed young woman, stood at the
foot of the stairs, ready to conduct the newly-
arrived party up to the chambers. She accordingly led the way, and Mr. George and the boys
followed — two neat-looking porters coming behind with the various articles of baggage.

The rooms were very pleasant apartments,
situated on the front side of the house, and looking out upon a beautiful square. The square

was enclosed in a high iron railing. It was
adorned with trees and shrubbery, and inter-
sected here and there with smooth gravel walks.
In the centre was a tall Doric column, with a
statue on the summit. There were other statues
in other parts of the square. One of them was
in honor of Watt, who is the great celebrity of
Glasgow — so large a share of the prosperity
and wealth of the whole region being due so
much to his discoveries.

"Now, boys," said Mr. George, "you will find
water and every thing in your room. Make
yourselves look as nice as a pin, and then go
down stairs and find the coffee room. When
you have found it, choose a pleasant table, and
order dinner. You may order just what you
please."

So Mr. George left the boys to themselves,
and went into his own room.

In about half an hour Rollo came up and told
Mr. George that the dinner was ready. So Mr.
George went down into the coffee room, Rollo
showing him the way.

Mr. George found that the boys had chosen a
very pleasant table indeed for their dinner. It
was in a corner, between a window and the fireplace. There was a pleasant coal fire in the fireplace, with screens before it, to keep the glow

of it from the faces of the guests. The room was quite large, and there was a long table extending up and down the middle of it, one of which is seen in the engraving. This table was set for dinner or supper. There were other smaller tables for separate parties in the different corners of the room.

Mr. George and the boys took their seats at the table.

" We thought we would have some coffee," said Rollo.

"That's right," said Mr. George. " I like coffee dinners. What else have you got ? "

" We have got some Loch Fine herring, and some mutton chops," said Rollo.

" Yes, sir," said Waldron. " You see the Loch Fine herrings are very famous, and we thought you would like to know how they taste."

By this time the waiter had removed the covers, and the party commenced their dinner. The fire, which was near them, was very pleasant, for although it was June the weather was damp and cold.

In the course of the dinner the boys introduced again the subject of going down the Clyde the next day.

"The boat goes from the Broomielaw," said Waldron.

THE COFFEE ROOM.

" The Broomielaw," repeated Mr. George ;
" what is the Broomielaw ? "

" Why, it is the harbor and pier," said Waldron. " It is below the lowest bridge. All the
boats that go down the river go from the Broomielaw. They go almost every hour. We can go
down by a boat and see the river, and then we
can come up by the railroad. That will be just
as cheap, if we take a second class car."

" Well, now," said Mr. George, " I have concluded that I should not be willing to have you
make this excursion except on two conditions ;
and they are such hard ones that I do not believe
you would accept them. You would rather not
go at all than go on such hard conditions."

" What are the conditions ? " asked Rollo.

" I don't believe you will accept them," said
Mr. George.

" But let us hear what they are," said Waldron. " Perhaps we should accept them."

" The first is," said Mr. George, " that when
you get home you must go to your room, and
write me an account of what you see on the excursion. Each of you must write a separate
account."

" That we will do," said Rollo. " I should
like to do that. Wouldn't you, Waldron ? "

Waldron seemed to hesitate. Though he was
a very active-minded and intelligent boy in

respect to what he saw and heard, he was somewhat backward in respect to knowledge of books and skill in writing. Finally, he said that he should be willing to *tell* Mr. George what he saw, but he did not think that he could write it.

"That is just as I supposed," said Mr. George. "I did not think you would accept my conditions."

"Well, sir, I will," said Waldron. "I will write it as well as I can. And what is the other condition?"

"That you shall write down, at the end of your account, the most careless thing that you see Rollo do, all the time that you are gone," said Mr. George, "and that Rollo shall write down the most careless thing he sees you do."

"But suppose we don't do any careless things at all," said Rollo.

"Then," said Mr. George, "you must write down what comes the nearest to being a careless thing. And neither of you must know what the other writes until you have shown the papers to me."

After some hesitation the boys agreed to both these terms, and so it was decided that they were to go down the river. The steamer which they were to take was to sail at nine o'clock, and so they ordered breakfast at eight. Mr. George said that he would go down with them in the morning to the Broomielaw, and see them sail.

CHAPTER V.

DOWN THE CLYDE.

THE boys returned in safety from their excursion about three o'clock in the afternoon. In fulfilment of their promise they immediately went to their room, and wrote their several accounts of the expedition. They agreed together that, in order to avoid repetitions, Waldron should dwell most upon the first part of the trip, and Rollo upon the last part.

The following is the account that Waldron wrote : —

"ACCOUNT OF OUR TRIP.

" First, there was a man standing by the plank, that asked us if we had got our tickets. We told him no. Then he showed us where to go and get them. It was at a little office on the pier. The price of the tickets was a shilling.

" The steamboat was not very large. There was no saloon on deck, and no awning, but only seats on deck, and many people sitting on them.

5

" There was a boy among them who had a kilt
on. It was the first kilt I ever saw.*

" We soon began to go down the river. The
sides of the river were walled up, to form piers,
all along, and there were a great many ships and
steamers moored to them. I saw several American vessels among them.

" By and by, when we got below the town, the
river grew wider, and the banks were sloping,
but they were paved all the way with large stones.
This was to prevent their being washed away by
the swell of the steamers. There were a great
many steamers going up and down, which kept
the water all the time a swashing against the
banks.

" I went up on the bridge where the captain
stood. There were good steps to go up, on the
side of the paddle box. Rollo would not go. I
had a fine lookout from the bridge. The captain
was there. He told me a good many things
about the river. He said that the river used to
be only five feet deep, and now it was almost

---

* It would have been better if Waldron had described the kilt;
but I suppose he thought he could not describe it very well. It
is a garment peculiar to the Scotch. It consists of a sort of sack
or jacket, with a skirt attached to it below, which comes down
just below the knees. The skirt is plaited upon the lower edge
of the jacket, and hangs pretty full.

twenty, all the way from the sea. They dug it out with dredging machines.

"I asked him what they did with the mud. He said they hauled it away, and spread it on the land in the country. They made a railroad, he said, on purpose to take the mud away to where it was wanted.

"Presently we began to come to the ship yards. There was an immense number of iron ships on the stocks, building. The workmen made a great noise with their hammers, heading the rivets. There seemed to be thousands of hammers going at a time.

"The steamers all sloped towards the water, and pointed down the stream. I suppose that this was so that when they were launched they might go down in the middle of the channel, and not strike the bank on the opposite side.

"We met a great many steamers coming up. One I thought had just been launched. She was full of workmen. There were a great many women running along on the bank, where it was green, trying to keep up with her. They were almost all barefooted. I suppose they had been down to see her launched. I wish we had been a little sooner.

"When I came down from the bridge I looked into the hold to see the engine. I wanted to go down, but I was afraid that Rollo would call it a careless thing. Besides, I could see pretty well where I was. There were three cylinders. Two acted alternately, and the other at the half stroke. I thought this was a very good plan ; for now the engine never can get on a poise. All these cylinders were inclined. The boiler was perpendicular. I never saw one like it before.

"After a while we got below the ship yards, and then there was nothing more to see, only some green grounds, and some mountains, and a castle on a rock. Then we landed at Greenock, and came home by the railroad. But Rollo is going to write about this.

"The most careless thing that Rollo did was that he came very near leaving his umbrella on board the boat at Greenock."

Rollo's account of the excursion was as follows : —

"EXCURSION ON THE CLYDE.

"Waldron and I went down the Clyde. We went on board the boat at the Broomielaw, in Glasgow.

"The first thing I observed was that a Scotchman and two boys came on board with violins and a flageolet, and began to play to amuse the company. At first I could not hear very well, the steampipe made such a noise. Afterwards, when the pipe stopped blowing off the steam, I could hear better, and I liked the music very well.

" By and by one of the boys came round to collect some money, and I put in a penny. I told Waldron that I thought he need not put in any thing, as he did not listen.

" There was a boat came off from the shore, and a man got out of it, and came on board our steamer just as we used to go on board the steamers on the Rhine. I wish we could go and travel on the Rhine again.

" When we got below the ships and ship yards we came to a part of the river where there were parks and pleasure grounds on the banks, and beautiful houses back among the trees.

" When we got half way down we stopped at a pier where there was a train of cars to take people to Loch Lomond, on the way to the Highlands. Waldron said that we should come there, he supposed, when we go to the Highlands.

" A little farther down we came to a great rocky hill, close by the water, with a castle upon it. The name of it is Dunbarton Castle. We shall go by it again, when we go to the Highlands.

"Then we came to a great widening of the river, and not long after that we arrived at Greenock and landed. We thought that the boat was going to stop here, but it did not. A great many of the passengers staid on board, and a great many more came on board, to go farther down the river.

"We went first to the station, so as to see when the trains went back to Glasgow. Then we took a walk.

"We found a street near the depot with a high hill behind it, and close to it. There were walls and terraces all the way up, and trees here and there. We looked up, and we could see the heads of some children over the topmost wall. They were looking down to where we were. Presently we came to an opening, and some flights of steps and steep walks, and so we thought we would go up.

"When we got to the top we found a broad terrace, with a wall along the front edge of it, where we could look down upon the river and the town. The town lay very narrow between the river and the foot of the hill. We were up very high above the tops of the houses.

"Behind us, on the terrace, were broad green fields and gravel walks, and beds of flowers, and great trees with seats under them. There were

a good many nursery maids around there, with
children. The nursery maids sat on the seats,
and the children played before them with the
pebbles and gravel.

"I read in the guide book about some famous
waterworks at Greenock, but we could not find
them. We asked one man, who was at work on
the gravel walks, if he could tell us where they
were; but he only stared at us and said he did
not 'knaw ony thing aboot it.'

"After this we went down the hill again, and
took a long walk along the bank of the river.
There was an omnibus going by, and we wanted
to get into it and see where it would carry us;
but we did not know but that it might carry us
to some place that we could not get back from
very soon. The name of the place where the
omnibus went was painted on the side of it
but it was a place that we had never heard of
before, and so we did not know where it was.

"After this we went back to the station, and
then came home. I thought from the map that
we should go through Paisley; but we did not.
We went _over_ it. We went over it, higher than
the tops of the chimneys.

"This is the end of my account; and the most
dangerous thing I saw Waldron do was to go up

on the bridge, on board the steamer, and talk there with the captain."

"Boys," said Mr. George, when he had finished reading these papers, "your accounts are excellent. The thing I chiefly like about them is, that you go right straight on and tell a plain story, without spoiling it all by making an attempt at fine writing. That is the way you ought always to write. One of these days I mean to get you both to write something for me in my journal."

CHAPTER VI.

WALKS ABOUT GLASGOW.

OUR party remained two days more in Glasgow, and visited quite a number of objects of interest and curiosity in and around the city.

At one end of the town there was a large open space, laid out for a pleasure ground; being somewhat similar in character to Boston Common, only it lay on the margin of the river, and commanded delightful views, both of the city itself and of the surrounding country. The grounds were adorned with trees and shrubbery, and paths were laid out over every portion of it, that were delightful to walk in. There were seats, too, at every point that commanded a pretty view. This place was called the Green.

The Green was at the eastern extremity of the city. At the other end, that is, towards the west, there was a region more elevated than the rest of the town, where the wealthy people resided. The streets were arranged in crescents and terraces, and were very magnificent. The houses

were almost all built of stone, and were of a
very massive and substantial, as well as elegant
character.

Nearer the centre of the town was a very large
and ancient church, called the cathedral. It was
a solemn-looking pile of buildings, standing by
itself in a green yard, back from the road, and
thousands of swallows were twittering and chirping high up among the pinnacles and cornices of
the roof. Although it was in the midst of a
crowded city, the whole structure wore an expression of great seclusion and solitude.

Behind the church, and separated from it by a
narrow valley, there was a steep hill, that was
covered, in every part, with tombs, and monuments, and sepulchral enclosures. The hill was
two or three hundred feet high, and there was a
very tall monument on the top of it. There was
a bridge across the valley behind the cathedral
leading to this cemetery.

"Ah," said Mr. George, "that is the Necropolis."

"The Necropolis?" repeated Rollo.

"Yes," said Mr. George. "I read about it in
the guide book. Necropolis means 'City of the
Dead,' and it is a city of the dead indeed."

There were pathways leading up the side of
the hill by many zigzags and windings. Across

the bridge leading to it was a great iron gateway, with a small iron gate open in the middle
of it. The boys wanted to go immediately to
the cemetery, in order to have the pleasure of
climbing up the zigzag paths to the top of the
hill. But Mr. George said he wished first to go
into the cathedral.

There was a gate leading into the cathedral
yard, and a porter's lodge just inside of it. There
was a sign up at the lodge, saying that the price
of admission to see the interior of the cathedral
was sixpence for each person. Waldron said
that he did not think it was worth sixpence to
go, and Rollo said that he did not care much
about going. He had seen cathedrals enough, he
said, on the continent. So it was agreed that the
boys should go to the cemetery, and wait there
till Mr. George came.

The boys accordingly went down the walk
that led to the bridge. They stopped a moment
at the open gate, not knowing whether it was
right for them to go in or not. As, however, the
gate was open, and there was nobody there to
forbid the passage, they stepped over the iron
threshold, and entered. There was a porter's
lodge just inside, and a man standing at the door
of it.

" Can we go in and see the cemetery ? " asked
Waldron.

" Certainly," said the porter. " Are you strangers in Glasgow ? "

" Yes, sir," said Rollo, " we are Americans.
My uncle is in the cathedral, and he is coming
pretty soon."

" Then please to come in," said the porter,
"and enter your names in the visitors' book."

So the boys went in. They found a very
pleasant room, with a large book open on a desk,
near a window. They wrote their names in this
book, and also their residences, and they stopped
a few minutes to look over the names that had
been written there before, in order to see if any
persons from America had recently visited the
cemetery. They found several names of persons
from New York on the list, and two or three
from Philadelphia. While the boys were looking
over the book the porter asked them a great
many questions about America.

In a few minutes they went on. They stopped
on the middle of the bridge, and looked down
over the balustrade into the ravine. The ravine
was very deep, and there was a little brook at
the bottom of it, and a sort of road or street
along the side of it, far below them.

The boys then went on into the cemetery. They
walked about it for some time, ascending continually higher and higher, and stopping at every
turn to read the inscriptions and monuments. At

length they reached the summit of the hill, where the lofty column stood which had been erected to the memory of John Knox, the great Scottish reformer. The column stood upon a pedestal, which contained an inscription on each of the four sides of it. One of these inscriptions said that John Knox was a man who could never be made to swerve from his duty by any fear or any danger, and that, although his life was often threatened by " dag and dagger," he was still carried safely through every difficulty and danger, and died, at last, in peace and happiness; and that the people of Glasgow, mindful of the invaluable services he rendered to his country, had erected that monument in honor of his memory.

The boys had just finished reading the inscription, when, looking down upon the bridge, they saw Mr. George coming. They went down to meet him, and then showed him the way up to the monument.

Mr. George first looked up to the summit of it, and then walked all around it, reading the inscriptions. He read them aloud, and the boys listened.

" Yes," said he, " John Knox was a true hero. He stood up manfully and fearlessly for the right when almost all the world was against him ; and to do that requires a great deal of courage, as

well as great strength of character. Many people reviled and hated him while he lived, but
now his memory is universally honored.

"I hope you two boys, when you come to be
men," continued Mr. George, "will follow his
example. What you know is right, that always
defend, no matter if all the world are against it.
And what is wrong, that always oppose, no matter if all the world are in favor of it."

"Yes, sir," said Waldron, "I mean to."

Mr. George and the boys rambled about the
Necropolis some time longer, and then went on.

While they were in Glasgow the party visited
several of the great manufacturing establishments.
They were all very much surprised at the lofti-
ness of some of the chimneys. There was one
at a great establishment, called the St. Rollox
Chemical Works, which was over four hundred
and thirty feet high, and Mr. George estimated
that it must have been thirty or forty feet diam-
eter at the base. If, now, you ask your father,
or some friend, how high the steeple is of the
nearest church to where you live, and multiply
that height by the necessary number, you will get
some idea of the magnitude of this prodigious
column. The lightning rod, that came down the
side of it in a spiral line, looked like a spider's
web that had been, by chance, blown against the
chimney by the wind.

CHAPTER VII.

ENTERING THE HIGHLANDS.

THE Highland district of Scotland occupies almost the whole of the western part of the island north of the valley of the Clyde. It consists of mountains, glens, and lakes, with roads winding in every direction through and among them. Of course the number of different Highland excursions which a tourist can plan is infinite. Most visitors to Scotland are, however, satisfied with a short tour among these mountains, on account of the great uncertainty of the weather. Indeed, as it rains here more than half the time, the chance is always in favor of bad weather; and the really pleasant days are very few.

The valley by which tourists from Glasgow most frequently go into the Highlands is the valley of Loch Lomond. The lower end of this lake comes to within about ten miles of the Clyde. The upper end of it extends about twenty-five miles into the very heart of the Highlands. There is an inn at the lower end of the lake, that is, the end nearest the Clyde, called Balloch Inn. At the upper end of the lake is another resting-place for travellers. A small steamboat passes every day through the lake, from one of these inns to the other, touching at various intermediate points on the way, at little villages or landing-places, where roads from the interior of the country come down to the lake.

From Balloch there is a railroad leading to the Clyde, though it does not extend to Glasgow. Travellers from Glasgow come down the Clyde in a steamer about ten miles to the railroad landing. There they take the cars, and proceed down the river, along the bank, amidst scenery of the grandest and most beautiful character, to Dunbarton Castle, where the road leaves the river, and turns into the interior of the country, towards the valley of Loch Lomond.

The road terminates at Balloch. Here the travellers are transferred to the steamer, and pursue their journey by water. It was this route Mr. George had determined to take on leaving Glasgow.

He got ready to leave Glasgow on the afternoon of a certain Thursday.

"Now, boys," said he, "we are ready to go to the Highlands. Find out for me when the boats and trains go, while I settle the bill."

So saying, Mr. George rose and rang the bell.

In Europe we do not go down to the office or bar room, when we are ready to leave a hotel, to call for and settle our bill there, as we do in America, but we ring the bell in our room, and ask the waiter to bring the bill to us.

"I have found out already," said Waldron. "There is a boat at four o'clock. It starts from the Broomielaw."

"And is there a train that connects with that boat?" asked Mr. George.

"Yes, sir," said Waldron.

"Then," said Mr. George, "we will go at four o'clock ; we shall just have time."

I am not certain that Waldron was entirely honest in giving this information to Mr. George, for he concealed one very important circumstance ; or rather he omitted to mention it. This circumstance was, that there was no boat from Balloch to connect with the train, so that if they were to go to Balloch that night, he knew that they could not go any farther till the next morning. He liked this, for he and Rollo had both begun to be tired of Glasgow, and he thought that if they should get to Balloch two or three hours before dark, there might be some chance for him and Rollo to go out fishing on the lake.

6

Very soon, however, he reflected that he should
enjoy his fishing less, if he resorted to any thing
like artifice or concealment to obtain it ; and
so, after a little hesitation, he frankly told Mr.
George that they could go no farther than to the
foot of the lake that night. There was only one
boat each day, he said, on the lake, and that left
Balloch in the morning, and returned at night.

Mr. George said that that made no difference.
He was tired of being in a great city, and would
like to see the country and the mountains again ;
and he should, therefore, prefer going to spend
the night at Balloch, rather than to remain in
Glasgow.

So the party set off. They embarked on board
the steamer at the Broomielaw. They ran rapidly down the river to the railroad landing.
They found the train waiting for them there, and
were whirled rapidly up the valley. There were
most charming views of the mountains on either
hand, with hamlets and villages scattered along
the slopes of them. At length they arrived at
Balloch. There was no village here, but only a
pretty inn, situated delightfully on the margin
of the lake, very near the outlet. There was an
elegant suspension bridge across the outlet, very
near the railroad station. There were several
thatch-covered cottages near, and two or three

castles were seen through openings among the trees on the hill-sides around. As the party crossed the suspension bridge, Rollo and Waldron, to their great delight, saw several boats floating in the water near the inn, and there was a boy on the bridge fishing over the railing. They stopped to talk with this boy, while Mr. George went on to engage rooms at the inn, and to order a supper.

When the boys came in they gave such fine accounts of the fishing on the lake, and of the facility with which they could obtain a boat, and a boatman to go out with them, that Mr. George was half persuaded to allow them to engage a boat, and to go out with them for an hour or two.

"And we want you to go with us, too," said Waldron, "if you can ; but if you have any thing else to do, we can go by ourselves, with the boatman."

"Yes," said Rollo, "and if you think it is not best for us to go at all, we can fish on the bridge."

Mr. George was much pleased to hear the boys speak in this manner in respect to the excursion. He was particularly glad to hear Waldron say that he desired that *he* should go with them. It is always an excellent sign when a boy wishes his father, or his mother, or his uncle, or whoever has the charge of him, to go with him, and share his pleasures ; and those parents and uncles who take an interest in the plans and enjoyments of their children, and sympathize with them in their feelings, in such a manner that the children like their company, place themselves in a position to exercise the highest possible influence over their conduct and character.

" Shall we have time ? " asked Mr. George.

" Yes, sir," said Waldron. " It is not dark here till half past ten, and it is only half past six now, so that there are four hours.

The farther you go north the longer the evenings are, in summer ; and at the time when our party made this visit to the Highlands, the evenings there were so long that you could see to read very well till nearly ten o'clock. The dawn, and the sunrise, too, come on proportionately early in the morning. The boys forgot this one morning, and finding that it was very light in their room when they woke, they got up, and dressed themselves, and went down stairs, thinking that it was nearly breakfast time. But they found, on looking at a clock in the hall of the inn, that it was not quite three o'clock !

But to return to the story.

Mr. George told the boys that if they would

Fishing on Loch Lomond.   Dialect of the Scottish boatmen.

arrange the boat party, that is, if they would engage the boat and the boatman, and also some
fishing lines, he would go with them. They
would have supper first, and then set out immediately afterwards.

This plan was carried into effect. Mr. George
himself cared nothing about the fishing. His
only object was to see the lake, and talk with
the Highland boatmen. Still he took a line and
fished a little, for company to the boys. The
excursion proved a very pleasant one. The lake
was beautiful. The surface of the water was
studded with pretty islands, and the shores were
formed of picturesque hills, which were every
where adorned with cottages, castles, groves,
fields, and all the other elements of rural beauty.

The excursion itself was very much like any
fishing excursion in America, only the peculiar
dialect of the boatman continually reminded the
travellers that they were in Scotland. For " I
don't know," he said "I dinna ken ;" for "trouble"
the word was "fash," and for " not," " na." The
boys had heard this phraseology before. The
railway porter, when he put Mr. George's valise
in the carriage, crowded it under the seat, where
he said it would not "fash the other travellers ; "
and at the inn, where Mr. George asked the ser-
vant girl if she would let them know when their

supper was ready, she said, "Yes, sir, I will coom
and tak ye doon."

Waldron enjoyed the fishing excursion very
much indeed. He said that he should like to
make the whole tour of Scotland in a boat, round
among the islands on the western and northern
shores. These islands are, indeed, very grand
and picturesque. They are groups of dark mountains, rising out of the sea. To cruise among
them in a yacht would be a very pleasant tour,
were it not for the incessant storms of wind and
rain to which the voyagers would be exposed.

Waldron said he particularly desired to go to
the Shetland Islands, on the north of Scotland,
in order to buy himself a pony.

" My father has promised me," said he, " that
if ever he goes to the Shetlands he will buy me a
pony."

" I should like a Shetland pony," said Rollo.

" Yes," said Waldron. " They are very hardy
animals, and then they are very docile and gentle. Some of them are as gentle and sagacious
as a dog. I read a story in a book once of one
that saved the life of a child, by plunging into
the water, and seizing the child by the clothes,
between his teeth, and bringing it safe to land.
The child fell into the water off of a steep bank,
and the horse jumped after it."

THE SHETLAND PONY.

Here is a picture of the horse which Waldron read about, climbing up the bank of the stream, bringing the child.

The party returned from the fishing excursion about eight o'clock ; but as it was still half an hour before sunset, Mr. George proposed to take a walk to one of the castles. The waiter at the hotel had told them that he could give them a ticket, and then the porter at the castle would let them in at the gate, and allow them to walk

about the grounds and around the castle, but
they could not go into it, for the proprietor and
his family were residing there.

Accordingly, when the party reached the landing, at the end of their excursion, they left the
boat, and walking across the bridge, they took
their course towards the castle. The road was
as smooth and hard as a floor, but it was bordered by close stone walls on either side, with
trees overhanging them. At length, after one or
two turnings, they came to the great gate which
led to the castle. The gateway was bordered
on each side with masses of trees and shrubbery,
and just within it was a small but very pretty
house, built of stone. This was the porter's
lodge. When they came up to the gate, and
looked through the bars of it, a little barefooted
girl came out from the door of the lodge, and
opened the gate to let them in.

On entering they found themselves at the com-
mencement of a smoothly gravelled avenue, which
led in a winding direction among the trees,
through a beautiful park. They walked on along
this avenue, supposing that it would lead them
to the castle. They passed various paths which
branched off here and there from the avenue, and
seemed to lead in various directions about the
grounds. The views which presented themselves

on every side were varied and beautiful. They saw several hares leaping about upon the grass — a sight which attracted the attention of the boys very strongly.

At length they came in sight of the castle. It stood on a swell of ground, at the foot of a high hill. The body of it consisted in part of a great round tower, with turrets and battlements above. The walls were covered with ivy.

After viewing the edifice as much as they wished, the party followed some of the winding walks, which led in various directions over the grounds ; and, though every thing had a finished and beautiful appearance, still the whole scene wore a very sombre expression.

" It must be a very solitary sort of grandeur, in my opinion," said Mr. George, " which a man enjoys by living in such a place as this."

" Why, I suppose he can have company if he wishes," said Rollo.

" Yes," said Mr. George. " Perhaps he lives in Edinburgh, or in London, in the winter, and in the summer he has company here. But then when he has company at all he must have them all the time, and he must have all the care and responsibility of entertaining them ; and that, I should think, would be a great burden."

Mr. George and the boys rambled over these

grounds about half an hour, and then they returned to the hotel. They were obliged to walk
fast the last part of the way, for dark, driving
clouds began to be seen in the sky, and just before they reached the hotel some drops of fine
rain began to fall.

" To-morrow is going to be a rainy day, I expect," said Rollo.

" Very likely," said Mr. George.

" And shall you go on over the lake if it is ? "
asked Rollo.

" I think we shall go as far as to the foot of
Ben Lomond," said Mr. George.

CHAPTER VIII.

ROWERDENNAN INN.

BEN LOMOND is one of the highest peaks
in Scotland. There are one or two that are
higher, but they are more remote, and conse-
quently less known. Ben Lomond is the one
most visited, and is, accordingly, the one that is
most renowned.

It lies on the east side of Loch Lomond, about
half way between the head of the lake and the
outlet. Our party were now at the outlet of the
lake, and were going the next morning towards
the head of it. The outlet of the lake is towards
the south. In this southern part, as I believe I
have already said, the lake is about ten miles
wide, and its banks are formed of hills and valleys of fertile land, every where well cultivated,
and presenting charming scenes of verdure and
fruitfulness. The lake, too, in this portion of it,
is studded with a great number of very picturesque and pretty islands.

As you go north, however, the lake, or loch, as

the Scotch call it, contracts in breadth, and the
land rises higher and higher, until at length you
see before you a narrow sheet of water, shut in
on either hand with dark and gloomy mountains,
the sides of which are covered every where with
ferns and heather, and seem entirely uninhabited.
They descend, moreover, so steep to the water
that there seems to be not even room for a path
between the foot of the mountains and the shore.

The highest peak of these sombre-looking hills
is Ben Lomond; which rises, as I have before
said, on the eastern side of the loch, about mid-
way between the head of the loch and the outlet.
At the foot of the mountain there is a point of
land projecting into the water, where there is an
inn. Tourists stop at this inn when they wish to
ascend the mountain. Other persons come to the
inn for the purpose of fishing on the loch, or of
making excursions by the footpaths which pene-
trate, here and there, among the neighboring
highlands. There is a ferry here, too, across the
loch. There is no village, nor, indeed, are there
any buildings whatever to be seen ; so that the
place is as secluded and solitary as can well be
imagined. It is known by the name of Rowerdennan Inn. It was at this point that Mr. George
proposed to stop, in case the day should prove
rainy.

When the boys rose the next morning, the first thing was to look out of the window, to see what the promise was in respect to the weather. It was not raining, but the sky was overcast and heavy.

"Good," said Waldron. "It does not rain yet, but it will before we get to Rowerdennan Inn."

Waldron was glad to see that there was a prospect of unfavorable weather, for he wished to stop at the inn. He had read in the guide book that they had boats and fishing apparatus there, and he thought that if they stopped perhaps another plan might be formed for going out on the loch a-fishing.

The steamer was to leave at nine o'clock. The boys could see her lying at the pier, about half a mile distant from them. The air was misty, and there were some small trees in the way, but the boys could see the chimney distinctly. They dressed themselves as soon as they could, and went to Mr. George's room. They knocked gently at the door. Mr. George said, "Come in." They went in and found Mr. George seated at a table, writing in his journal. It was about seven o'clock.

Mr. George laid aside his writing, and after bidding the boys good morning, and talking with

them a few minutes about the plans of the day,
took a testament which he had upon a table
before him, and read a few verses from one of
the Gospels, explaining the verses as he read
them. Then they all knelt down together, and
Mr. George made a short and simple prayer, ask-
ing God to take care of them all during the day,
to guard them from every danger, to make them
kind and considerate towards each other, and
towards all around them, and to keep them from
every species of sin.

This was the way in which Mr. George always
commenced the duties of the day, when travelling with Rollo, whether there were any other
persons in company or not ; and a most excellent
way it was, too. Besides the intrinsic propriety
of coming in the morning to commit ourselves to
the guardian care and protection of Almighty
God, especially when we are exposed to the vicis-
situdes, temptations, and dangers that are always
hovering about the path of the traveller in foreign lands, the influence of such a service of
devotion, brief and simple as it was, always
proved extremely salutary on Rollo's mind, as
well as on the minds of those who were associ-
ated with him in it. It made them more gentle,
and more docile and tractable ; and it tended
very greatly to soften those asperities which we

often see manifesting themselves in the inter-
course of boys with each other.

When the devotional service was finished, Mr.
George sent the boys down stairs, to make arrangements for breakfast. In about half an hour
Rollo came up to say that breakfast was ready in
the coffee room, and Mr. George went down.

After breakfast Mr. George took the valise,
and the boys took the other parcels of baggage,
and they all went over the bridge to the railway
station. They waited here a short time, until at
length the train came. They would have walked
on to the pier, where the boat in which they
were going to embark was lying, but it was beginning to rain a little, and Mr. George thought
it would be better to wait and go in the cars.
The distance was not more than a quarter of a
mile, and the boys were quite curious to know
what the price of the tickets would be, for such
a short ride. They found that they were three-
pence apiece.

The train came very soon, bringing with it
several little parties of tourists, that were going
into the Highlands. They all seemed greatly
chagrined and disappointed at finding that it
was beginning to rain.

When the train stopped opposite the pier, the
passengers hurried across the pier, and over the

plank, on board the boat. The rain was falling
fast, and every thing was dripping wet. The
gentlemen went loaded with portmanteaus, carpet
bags, valises, and other parcels of baggage, while
the women hurried after them, holding their umbrellas in one hand, and endeavoring, as well as
they could, to lift up their dresses with the other.
The boat was very small, and there was no shelter whatever from the rain on the deck. Most
of the company, therefore, hurried down into the
cabin.

"Are you going down into the cabin, too,
uncle George?" said Rollo.

"Not I," said Mr. George. "Rain or no rain,
I am going to see the shores of Loch Lomond."

There was a heap of baggage near the centre
of the boat, covered with a tarpauling. Mr.
George put his valise and the knapsacks under
the covering, with the other travellers' effects,
and then began to look about for seats. There
was a range of wooden benches all along the
sides of the deck, but they were very wet, and
looked extremely uncomfortable. The water,
however, did not stand upon them, for they were
made of open work, on purpose to let the water
through.

"If we only had some camp stools," said Mr.
George, " we could get sheltered seats under the

lee of the baggage; but as it is, we must make the best of these."

VIEWING THE SCENERY OF LOCH LOMOND.

So he folded his shawl long enough to make a cushion for three persons, and laid it down on one of the benches. He sat down himself upon the centre of it, and the boys took their places on each side. Mr. George then spread his umbrella, and the boys, by sitting very close to him,

7

could both come under it. By the time they
were thus established the boat had left the pier,
and was gliding smoothly away over the waters
of the lake, with green and beautifully wooded
islands all around. In the distance up the lake,
wherever the opening of the clouds afforded a
view, it was seen that the horizon was bounded,
and the waters of the lake were shut in, with
dark and gloomy-looking mountains, the summits
of which were entirely concealed from view.

After a short time the rain increased, and all
the scenery, except such islands and portions of
the shore as came very near the track of the
steamer, was soon entirely hidden. The wind
blew harder, too, and drove the rain in under
the umbrella, so that our travellers were beginning to get quite wet.

"Suppose I go below," said Waldron, "and see
what sort of a place the other passengers have
found down there."

" Yes, sir," said Rollo; " it is so wet here, and
besides, I am beginning to be cold."

" We will all go," said Mr. George.

So they all went below. They descended one
at a time, by a small spiral staircase, near the
stern, which led them into the cabin of the boat.
The cabin presented to view quite an extraordinary spectacle.

It was a small room, being not much more
than fifteen feet wide. Along the sides of it
were seats made of carved oak, and very comfort-
ably cushioned. Above was a row of small
windows, through which you could look out by
kneeling on the seats. At the end of the cabin
were a fireplace and a grate. There was a
coal fire burning in the fireplace, and several of
the passengers were hovering around it to warm
and dry themselves. Others were looking out
of the windows, vainly endeavoring to obtain
some glimpses of the scenery. A great many of
them were uttering exclamations of disappointment and vexation, at finding all the pleasure
of their excursion spoiled thus by the cold and
the rain.

Some of the travellers, however, more philo-
sophical than the rest, seemed to take their ill
luck quite patiently. There was one group that
opened their knapsacks at one of the side tables,
and were taking breakfast together there in a
very merry manner.

Mr. George and the two boys went to the fire,
and stood there to warm themselves, listening, in
the mean time, to the exclamations and remarks
of the various groups of passengers, which they
found quite amusing. In the mean time the
steamer went on, bringing continually new points

of land and new islands into view. She stopped, too, now and then, at landings along the margin of the lake ; and on these occasions Rollo and Waldron always went up on deck, to witness the operation of bringing the steamer to, and to see who went on shore.

They had a list of these landings on the tickets which they had bought of the captain of the boat, as soon as they came on board. When they found that the next landing was Rowerdennan, all the party went up on deck. The rain, they now found, had ceased. Indeed, the sky looked quite bright, and several of the passengers were standing on the wet deck, watching for glimpses of the mountains, which appeared here and there through the openings in the clouds. They saw repeatedly the dark and gloomy sides of Ben Lomond ; but a canopy of dense and heavy clouds rested upon and concealed the summit.

The boys obtained a glimpse of a stone house, nearly enveloped in trees, at a little distance from the shore, as they approached the land. This they supposed was the inn, as there was no other house in sight.

The steamer drew up to the pier. The pier was very small. It was built of timbers, and extended a little way out over the water, from a

solitary place on the shore. Every passenger
that left the boat had to pay twopence for the
privilege of landing upon it. The porter of the
inn stood there, with a leather bag hung over his
neck, to collect this toll. On this occasion, however, he got only sixpence, as Mr. George and
the two boys were the only passengers that
landed.

The place was very wild and solitary. There
was no house, or building of any kind, in sight.
There was a narrow road, however, that led
along the shore of the lake, from the pier towards the point of land which the steamer had
passed in coming to the pier, and the porter told
Mr. George that that was the road that led to
the inn.

"If you will walk on," said the porter, "I will
bring your luggage."

There were some boards and small timbers on
the deck of the vessel, which were to be landed
here, and the porter remained in order to receive
them, while Mr. George and the boys went on.
They soon came to the inn. They entered it
from behind, through a very pleasant yard, surrounded with trees and gardens, and out-build-
ings of various kinds. Mr. George went in,
followed by the boys, and was shown into the
coffee room. From the windows of this room

there was a very pretty view of the lake, through
an opening among the trees of the garden.

"And now what are we going to do?" said
Waldron, after they had all looked at the view
as much as they wished.

"I am going to have a fire," said Mr. George,
"and then sit down here and make myself comfortable until it clears away. You and Rollo can
join me, or you can form any other plan that you
like better."

"We'll go a-fishing," said Waldron.

"Or else go up on Ben Lomond," said Rollo.
"How high is Ben Lomond, uncle George?"

"It is between three and four thousand feet,"
said Mr. George. "We will all go up to-morrow
if it clears away."

But Waldron did not wish to go up the mountain. He preferred to go a-fishing on the lake.
He did not express his preference very strongly
at this time, but in the course of the afternoon
he persuaded Rollo that it would be a great deal
better for them to go out a-fishing on the lake,
and perhaps go across the lake to the opposite
shore, rather than to go up the mountain; and
he induced Rollo to join him in a request that
Mr. George would let them go out on the lake,
while he went up the mountain, if he wished to
ascend it.

"We can have a boat and a boatman," said Waldron. "The boatman will row us, and take care of us, and that will be perfectly safe. And Rollo would like that plan best, too."

In forming this scheme Waldron and Rollo made a mistake ; and it was a mistake that boys are very apt to fall into when they are invited to go on excursions with their parents, or uncles, or older brothers. It is naturally to be supposed that the tastes and inclinations of boys, in such cases, should often be different from those of the grown persons they are with, and should lead them to wish frequently to deviate, more or less, from the plans formed. But it is a great source of inconvenience to those whom they are with to have them often propose such deviations. In this case, for example, Mr. George had come a long distance, and incurred very heavy expenses, for the purpose of seeing the Scottish Highlands. Unless he could now really see them, of course all his time and money would be lost. The pleasure of going a-fishing is, doubtless, often very great, but this was not the time nor the place for enjoying it. In acceding to the arrangement to come with Mr. George to the Highlands, the boys ought to have considered themselves joined with him in a tour for instruction and improvement, and as committed to the plans which he might form, from time to time, for accomplishing the objects of the tour. By proposing, as they did, to deviate on every occasion from these plans, and wishing to turn aside from the proper duty of tourists, in search of such boyish pleasures as might be enjoyed just as well at home, they failed signally in fulfilling the obligations which they incurred in undertaking the tour under Mr. George's charge.

Let all the boys and girls, therefore, who read this book, remember that whenever, either by invitation or otherwise, they are joined to any party of which a grown person has charge, or when they accompany a grown person on any excursion whatever, they go to share *his* pleasures, not to substitute their own for his, and thus to interfere with and thwart the plans which he had formed. Boys often violate this rule from want of thought, and without intending to do any thing wrong. This was the case in this instance, in respect to Waldron and Rollo.

" They are good boys," said Mr. George to himself, in thinking of the subject. " They do not mean to do any thing wrong ; but they do not understand the case. I will take an opportunity soon to explain it to them."

It is no time, however, to explain to a boy why it is not best that he should do a particular

Conditions.   The proposal agreed to.

thing, when he wishes to do it and you forbid
him. His mind is then too much occupied with
his disappointment, and perhaps with vexation,
to listen to the reasons. Forbid him, if it is
necessary to do so, but reserve the explanation
till some future time.

Mr. George got over the difficulty in this case
in a very pleasant manner to all concerned. The
rain ceased entirely about noon, but the paths on
the mountain he knew would be too wet to make
it agreeable to ascend that day; so he told the
boys that if they would find the boat and the
man, and make all the arrangements, he would
go out with them on the lake; and that, if they
would agree to write a chapter for his journal,
and write it as well as they had written their
accounts of their excursion to Greenock, he
would stop an hour on the way, to let them fish.

"And then," said he, "we'll all ascend the
mountain together to-morrow."

This proposal was readily agreed to on the
part of the boys, and the compact was accordingly made. They engaged the boat and the
man, and after dinner they all three embarked.
The rain had ceased, but the sky was covered
with clouds, and heavy masses of mist were
driving along the sides and over the summits of
the mountains. The weather, however, remained

tolerably favorable until the boat had nearly
reached the opposite shore of the lake ; but then
a dense mass of clouds came down from the
mountains on the eastern side, and the whole
shore was soon concealed from view by the
driving scuds and the falling rain. The boatman pulled hard to reach the shore before the
shower should come on. The gust overtook
them, however, when they were about a quarter
of a mile from the landing. Fortunately the wind,
though very violent, was fair, and it drove them
on towards the shore. Mr. George and the boys
sat down in the bottom of the boat, at the stern,
and spreading a large umbrella behind them,
they sheltered themselves as well as they could
from the wind and the rain. The poor boatman
got very wet.

They found shelter when they reached the
land, and soon the shower passed away. Then,
after rambling about a short time among the
huts and cottages of the village where they
landed, they set out again on their return. They
stopped to fish at a short distance from the shore
on the eastern side, and were quite successful.
The boys caught several trout, which they re-
solved to have fried for their breakfast the next
morning. While they were fishing Mr. George
sat in the stern of the boat, studying his guide

books, and learning all he could about the remarkable events in the life of Rob Roy, the
great Highland chieftain, who formerly lived on
the shores of Loch Lomond, and performed many
daring exploits there, which have given him a
great name in Scottish history.

It was a little after nine o'clock when they
returned to the inn.

The next morning the plan of ascending the
mountain was carried into effect. Mr. George
hired two horses, intending to take turns with
the boys in riding them. By having two horses
for three riders, each one could, of course, ride
two thirds of the way. This is better than for
each one to ride all the way, as that is very tire-
some. Both in ascending and descending mountains it relieves and rests the traveller to walk a
part of the way.

The top of the mountain was distinctly in
sight from the inn, and almost the whole course
of the path which led up to it, for there were no
woods to intercept the view. The distance was
five or six miles. The path was a constant and
gradual ascent nearly all the way, and lay
through a region entirely open in every direction. There was a perfect sea of hills on every
side, all covered with moss, ferns, and heather,
with scarcely a tree of any kind to be seen,

except those that fringed the shores of the lake
down in the valley. The view from the summit
was very extended, but the wind blew there so
bleak and cold that the whole party were very
glad to leave it and come down, after a very
brief survey of the prospect.

In coming down the mountain the party
stopped at a spring, to rest themselves and to
drink ; and here, as they were sitting together
on the flat stones that lay about the spring, Mr.
George explained to the two boys what I have
already explained in this chapter to the reader,
in respect to the duty of boys, when travelling
under the charge of a grown person, to fall in
with their leader's plans, instead of forming independent plans of their own.

" When you are at home," said he, " and playing among yourselves, and with other persons of
your own age, then you can form your own plans,
and arrange parties and excursions for just such
purposes and objects as you think will amuse you
most. But we are now travelling for improvement, not for play. We are making a tour in
Scotland for the purpose of learning all we can
about Scotland, with a view to obtain more full
and correct ideas respecting it than we could obtain by books alone. So we must attend to our
duty, and be content with such enjoyments and

such pleasures as come in our way, and not turn aside from our duty to seek them."

The boys both saw that this was reasonable and right, and they promised that thenceforth they would act on that principle.

"We won't ask to go a-fishing again all the time we are in Scotland," said Waldron.

"That's right," said Mr. George. "And now as soon as we get to the hotel it will be time for the boat to come along; and all the rest of our adventures to-day you and Rollo must write an account of, to put into my journal. You will not write the account till you get to Stirling; but you had better take notice of what we do, and what we see, so as to be ready to write it when we arrive."

"May we take notes?" asked Rollo.

"Certainly," said Mr. George. "That will be an excellent plan. Have a small piece of paper and a pencil at hand, and when you see any thing remarkable, make a memorandum of it. That will help you very much when you come to write."

This plan was carried into effect. The boys wrote their account, and after it was duly corrected it was carefully transcribed into Mr. George's journal. It was as follows. Rollo wrote one half of it, and Waldron the other.

110   ROLLO IN SCOTLAND.

The Trossachs.   The boys' account of their tour.

CHAPTER IX.

THE TOUR OF THE TROSSACHS.

" THE Trossachs is the name of a narrow gorge among the mountains. It begins at the end of a lake, and extends about two or three miles. The sides are covered with forests, and there are high, sharp rocks seen every where, peeping out among the trees.

" The pass of the Trossachs is not in the same valley that Loch Lomond lies in, but in another valley almost parallel to it, about five miles off. There is high land between. We had to cross this high land on foot, or in a carriage. The plan was to go up the lake a few miles farther, to a landing called Inversnaid, and there leave the boat, and go across the mountains.

" When it was nearly time for the boat to come, we took our valise and other things, and walked along the shore path till we came to the pier. We overtook some other people who were going in the boat, too. A soldier came along, also. He was one of the sappers and miners, that we saw on the top of Ben Lomond. He told me that he came down to get some things that were coming in the boat.*

"We waited on the pier a few minutes, and then we saw the boat coming around a point of land. As soon as she came up to the pier we all got in, and a gentleman and two ladies came on shore.

"The weather was very pleasant, and so we did not go down into the cabin. All the passengers were on the deck, looking at the mountains. I talked with some of them. One party came from New York, and the gentleman asked me what there was to see at Rowerdennan Inn; and so I told him about our going across the lake, and about our ascending the mountain. He said he wished that he had landed, too, so that he might go up the mountain, since it proved to be such a pleasant day.

"Uncle George gave Waldron and me leave to go up on the bridge to see the mountains before us, up the lake. They looked very dark and gloomy. The captain was there. He told

---

* The boys had seen a party of sappers and miners, as they are called, that is, military engineers, who were established on the top of Ben Lomond, in a hut which they had built there. They were employed there, in connection with other sappers and miners on the other mountains around, in making a survey of Scotland.

us the names of the mountains that were in sight.
He said that when we landed at Inversnaid we
should go across the high land, and then should
come to another lake, where there was another
steamboat, only she had not commenced her trips
yet, and so we should have to go down the other
lake in a row boat.   Waldron and I were both
glad of that.

THE BOYS ON THE BRIDGE.

"At last we came to Inversnaid. We thought
it would be a town, but it was not. It was only
an inn on the slope of the mountain, near the
shore, and by the side of a waterfall. We
walked up a steep path to the inn, from the pier.
We had to pay twopence apiece for the privilege of landing on the pier. Uncle George
asked us whether we would rather walk or ride
across the high land to the other valley. We
said we did not care. He said that he would
rather ride. So he engaged one of the *machines*.
They call the carriages machines. There were
two standing in the inn yard. There were two
seats to these carriages, but no top, and very little room for any baggage. So it was lucky for
us that we had so little.

"While the hostler was harnessing the horse
we went to see the waterfall. There was a path
leading to it through the bushes. There was a
small foot bridge over the stream, just below the
waterfall, where we could stand and see the
water tumbling down over the rocks.

"While we were there they called us to tell us
that the machine was ready. So we went back
to the inn. There were two machines ready at
the door. One was for another party. There
was a lady in that machine, and it was just starting. Ours was just starting, too. They told us

8

that there was a steep hill at the beginning, and that it was customary for the gentlemen to walk up.

" So we walked up. The road lay along the brink of a deep ravine, with the brook that made the waterfall tumbling along over the rocks at the bottom of it.

" When we got to the top of the hill the machine stopped, and we all got in. Waldron rode on the front seat with the driver, and uncle George and I rode behind.

" The country was very wild and dreary. There was nothing to be seen all around but hills and mountains, all covered with brakes and ferns, and moss and heather. There were no woods, no pastures, no fields, and no farm houses. It was the dreariest-looking country I ever saw. In the middle of the way we came to some old stone hovels, with thatched roofs — very dismal-looking dwellings indeed. There was usually one door and one little window by the side of it. The window was about as big as you would make for a horse, in the side of a stable. I looked into one of these hovels. There was no floor, only flat stones laid in the ground, and scarcely any furniture. The Irish shanties, where they are making railroads in America, are very pretty houses compared to them.

" The driver told us that the whole country belonged to a duke. He keeps it to shoot grouse in, in the fall of the year. The grouse is a bird like a partridge. They live on the heather. I saw some of them flying about.

" The road was very good. The duke made it, the driver said. We could see the road a great way before us, along the valley. By and by we saw some people coming. They were a great way off, but we could see that they were travellers, by the umbrellas, and shawls, and knapsacks they had in their hands. Presently we could see a man coming up a hill just before them with a wheelbarrow load of trunks that he was wheeling along. So we knew that it was a party of travellers, coming across from Loch Katrine to Loch Lomond; but we wondered why they did not take a machine, and ride.

" When we came up to them we stopped a moment to talk to them. There were two gentlemen and two ladies. One of the ladies looked pretty tired. They said that there were no machines on the side of the mountain where they came from, and that there was a party there, that arrived before them, who had engaged the first machines that should come; and so they were obliged to walk, and to have their trunks wheeled over on a wheelbarrow.

" Afterwards we met another party walking

in the same way, with their trunks on a wheel-barrow. We thought that five miles was a great way to wheel trunks on a wheelbarrow.

" At last we came to what they called Loch Katrine ; but it seemed to me nothing but a pond among the mountains. It was only about ten miles long. There was an inn on the shore, but no village.

" There was a pier there, too, and some boats drawn up on the beach. At a little distance they were putting together an iron steamboat on the stocks. The parts were all made in Glasgow, and brought here by the same way that we had come. The old steamboat of last year was float-ing in the water near by. The steam pipe was rusty, and she looked as if she had been aban-doned. The name of her was the Rob Roy.

" We were glad that the new one was not ready, for we liked better to go in a row boat.

" So we engaged one of the boats, and went down to it on the beach, and put our baggage in. And this is the end of my part of the account. Waldron is to write the rest.

" ROLLO."

" We all got into the boat ; that is, we three, and some other ladies and gentlemen that came over the mountain about the same time with us.

The wind was blowing pretty fresh, and the middle of the lake was very rough, and some of the ladies were afraid to go ; but we told them there was no danger.

"The boatman said that we would go right across the loch, and then we should get under the lee of the land on the eastern shore, and there we should be sheltered from the wind, and the water would be smooth.

" I told him that I could row, and asked him to let me take one of the oars ; and he said I might. But one of the ladies was afraid to have me do it. She said she was afraid that I should upset the boat.

" This was nonsense ; for it is not possible to upset a boat by any kind of rowing, if it is ever so bad.

" The boatman told her that there was no danger, and that, if I could really row, I could help him so much that we should get across the part of the lake where the wind blew and the waves run high so much the sooner. So she consented at last, and I took one of the oars, and we rowed across the loch in fine style. We pitched about a good deal in the middle passage, and the lady was dreadfully frightened ; but when we got across. the water became smooth, and we sailed very pleasantly along the shore.

" The shores were winding and very pretty, and the farther we went the narrower the lake became, and the mountains became higher and higher. At last we came to a narrow place between two mountains, where the pass of the Trossachs began. The mountain on one side was Ben Venue. The one on the other side was Benan. The shores at the foot of these mountains were covered with woods, and the place was very wild. There was an island in the middle of the lake here, called Ellen's Isle. This island was high and rocky, and covered with woods, like the shores adjacent to it.

" This island is very famous, on account of a poem that Walter Scott wrote about it, called the Lady of the Lake. The lake was this Loch Katrine, and the lady was Ellen. She went back and forth to the island in a boat, in some way or other, but I do not know the story exactly. Mr. George is going to buy the Lady of the Lake when we get to Edinburgh, and read it to us, and then we shall know.

" The island is small and rocky, but it is so covered with trees and bushes that we hardly see the rocks. They peep out here and there. The banks rise very steep, and the water looks very deep close to the shore. We sailed by the island, and then the water grew narrower and narrower, until at last we were closely shut in, and then soon we came to the landing.

"There was nothing but a hut at the landing, and a narrow road, which began then and led down the valley. The valley was very narrow, and there were steep rocks and mountains on both sides. They told us that it was a mile and a quarter to the inn, and that there was no other way to go but to walk. The boatman said that he would bring the baggage; so we left it under his care, all except our knapsacks, and walked along.

"We walked about a mile down the valley, by a very winding road, with rocks, and trees, and very high mountains on both sides. At last we came in sight of a tall spire. I thought it was a church. In a minute another spire came into view, and two great towers. Rollo thought it was a castle. I said that a castle would not have a spire on it. Rollo said that a church would not have two spires on it. It turned out that both of us were mistaken; for the building was the inn.

"It was a very extraordinary looking inn. It was built of stone, with towers and battlements, like an old castle. The inside was very extraordinary, too. The public room looked, as Mr. George said, like an old Gothic hall of the mid-

dle ages. There were tables set out here for
people to have breakfasts and dinners, and Mr.
George ordered a dinner for us. There were
other parties of tourists there, some coming, and
some going.

"While the dinner was getting ready, Rollo
and I walked about the inn, and in the yards. It
was a very curious place indeed. Close behind
it were lofty mountains, which, Rollo said, looked
like the mountains of Switzerland ; only there
were no snow peaks on the top of them. There
was no village, and there were no houses near,
except two or three stone hovels in the woods
behind the inn. Before the inn, in a little valley
just below it, was a pond, such as they call here
a loch.

"Mr. George decided to go directly on to
Stirling, because it was Saturday night, and he
did not wish, he said, to spend Sunday at such a
lonesome inn. So we hired a carriage and set off.
Immediately we began to come out from the
mountains, and to get into the level country.
The country soon grew very beautiful. The sun
was behind our backs, and it shone right upon
every thing that we wished to see, and made the
whole country look very green and very bril-
liant. There were parks, and gardens, and
pleasure grounds, and queer villages, and ruins

of old castles on the hills, and little lochs in the valleys, and every thing beautiful.

"At last we came in sight of Stirling Castle. It stood on the top of a high, rocky hill. The hill was very high and steep on all sides but one, where it sloped down towards the town. The country all around was very level, so that we could see the castle a great many miles away.

"We rode around the foot of the castle hill, under the rocks, and at last came into the town, and drove to the hotel.

"WALDRON."

CHAPTER X.

STIRLING.

STIRLING Castle crowns the summit of a rocky hill, which rises on the banks of the Forth, in the midst of a vast extent of level and richly-cultivated country.   It is, of course, a very conspicuous object from all the region around.

The hill is long and narrow.   The length of it extends from north to south.   The northern end is the high end.   The land slopes gently towards the south, but the other sides are steep, and in many places they form perpendicular precipices of rock, with the castle walls built on the very brink of them.

The town lies chiefly at the foot of the hill, towards the south, though there are one or two streets, bordered by quaint and queer old buildings, that lead all the way up to the castle.

In front of the castle, at the place where these streets terminate, is a broad space, smoothly gravelled, called the esplanade.   This is used as a parade ground, for drilling and training the new soldiers, and teaching them the manœuvres and exercises necessary to be practised in the war.

On Sunday morning, after breakfast, Mr. George and the boys went out, to go to church. Bells were ringing in various parts of the town. They were drawn, by some invisible attraction, up the hill, in the direction of the castle. They soon found other people going the same way; and following them, they came, at length, to a very ancient-looking mass of buildings, which, Mr. George said, he should have thought was an old abbey, gone to ruin, if it were not that the people were all going into it, under a great arched doorway. So he supposed it was a church, and he and the boys went in with the rest.

There was a man at the door holding a large silver plate, to receive the contributions of the people that came in. Mr. George stopped to get some money out of his pocket. The man then seemed to perceive that he was a stranger; so he said to him, speaking with a broad Scotch accent and intonation, —

"Ye wull gae into the magistrates' seat. Or stay — I wull send a mon wi' ye, to show ye the wa'."

So he called a door keeper, and the door keeper led the way up stairs, into a gallery. The gal-

lery was very wide, and was supported by enormous pillars. The whole interior of the church
had a very quaint and antique air. The magis-
trate's seat was the front seat of the gallery. It
was a very nice seat, and was well cushioned.
Before it, all around, was a sort of desk, for the
Bibles and Hymn Books to rest upon.

There were three pulpits — or what seemed to
the boys to be pulpits — one behind and above
the other. The highest was for the minister;
the next below was for what in America would
be called the leader of the choir; though in Scotland, Mr. George said he believed he was called
the precentor. There was no choir of singers,
as with us, but when the minister gave out a
hymn the precentor rose and commenced the
singing, and when he had got near the end of
the first line all the congregation joined in, and
sang the hymn with him to the end. The third
pulpit was only a sort of chair, enclosed at the
sides and above. What the man did who sat in
it the boys could not find out.

All the people in the church had Bibles on a
sloping board before them, in their pews, and
when the minister named the text or read a
chapter, they all turned to the place, and looked
over. Waldron said he thought that this was
an excellent plan.

Mr. George and the boys all liked the sermon very much indeed, and when the service was ended, they walked a little way around the esplanade before the castle, and then went home to dinner.

In the course of their excursion, however, they had observed that a great many walks had been made at different elevations on the west side of the hill, and that seats were placed there at different points, for resting-places. These seats, and indeed the walks themselves, commanded charming views of all the surrounding country. The boys wanted to run up and down these paths, and explore the sides of the hill by means of them in every part; but Mr. George recommended to them to wait till the next day.

"We shall come up to-morrow," said he, "to visit the castle, and then we will come out here, and have a picnic, on one of these stone seats. After that I will find a place among the rocks to read or write, for an hour, and while I am there you may climb about among the rocks and precipices as much as you please."

The next morning the boys set out with Mr. George, soon after breakfast, to go up to the castle. When they reached the esplanade they found several small parties of soldiers there, under instruction. They all wore red coats —

that being the ordinary uniform of British soldiers. Officers were marching them about, and
teaching them how to handle their muskets, and
to keep step, and to wheel this way and that, and
to perform other such evolutions. A great many
of the soldiers looked very young. They were
lads that had been recently enlisted, and were
now being trained to go to the war in the Crimea.

After looking at these soldiers a short time
the party went on. At the upper end of the
esplanade there was a gateway leading into the
castle yard. There was a sentinel, in a Highland
costume, keeping guard there. Mr. George asked
him if the public were allowed to go into the
castle. He said, " O, yes, certainly ; " and so Mr.
George and the boys went in.

As they went in they looked up, and saw a
great many cannons pointed down at them from
the embrasures in the surrounding ramparts and
bastions.

" Those guns must be to keep the enemy from
coming in," said Waldron.

Presently the party passed through another
arched gateway, and came into a large inner
court, which was surrounded with various buildings, all built of stone, and of a very massive
and solid character. The palace was on one
side. It was adorned with a great many quaint

and curious sculptures and images. The palace
itself, and all the other buildings, were used as
barracks for soldiers. A great many soldiers
were standing about the doors, and some were
playing together about the court. Some of them
were dressed in the common British uniform, and
some were in the Highland costume.

While the boys were looking at the palace
front, a soldier advanced towards them in a very
respectful manner, and said to Mr. George, —

"If you and the young gentlemen are strangers
in Stirling, I will walk about the castle with
you, and point out the objects of interest to you,
if you desire it."

Mr. George accepted this offer, and the young
soldier accordingly walked with them all about.
He pointed out all the different buildings, and
mentioned the dates of the erection of them, and
referred to the most important historical events
that had transpired in them. Finally he led the
party through a gate into a small garden, and
thence out upon the rampart wall, from which
there was a very extended and extraordinarily
beautiful view of the surrounding country.* To
the north-west were seen the Highlands, with the
peaks of Ben Lomond, Ben Venue, and Benan,

* For engraving of Stirling Castle see page 10.

rising conspicuously among them. On the east were other hills, rising abruptly out of the smooth and smiling plain, and covered with dark plantations of evergreen. All around the foot of the castle, and extending to the distance, in some directions, of many miles, the country was level and fertile, and it presented every where the most enchanting pictures of rural beauty. Some of the fields were of the richest green, others were brown from fresh tillage, with men ploughing or harrowing in them, or plants just springing up in long green rows, which, partly on account of the distance, and partly through the exquisite neatness and nicety of farmers' work, looked so smooth, and soft, and fine, that the scene appeared more like enchantment than reality.

On one side of the mountain was seen the River Forth, winding about through meadows and green fields with the most extraordinary turnings and involutions. The boys had seen winding rivers before, but never any thing like this. The whole plain was filled with the windings of the river, which looked like the links of a silver chain, lying half embedded in a carpet of the richest green. Indeed, these windings of the river, and the vast circular fields of fertile land which they enclose, are called the Links of Forth. The view was diversified by villages, hamlets,

bridges, railway embankments, and other con-
structions, which concealed the river here and
there entirely from view, and made it impossible
to trace its course. The richness and beauty of
these Links of Forth appeared the more surprising
to the boys from the contrast which the scene
presented to the dreary wastes of moss and
heather which they had seen in the Highlands.
There is an old Scotch proverb that refers to this
contrast. It is this : —

> " The lairdship of the bonnie Links of Forth
> Is better than an *earldom* in the north."

The course of the Forth could be traced for a
long distance towards Edinburgh ; and Arthur's
Seat, a high hill near Edinburgh, could be distinctly seen in the south-eastern horizon.

At one place, in an angle in the wall of the
rampart, was a stone step, so placed that a lady,
by standing upon it, might get a better view.
The soldier said that Queen Victoria stood upon
that stone, when she visited Stirling Castle, a
few years ago, on her way to Balmoral. Balmoral is a country seat she has among the Highlands, far to the north, in the midst of the wildest
solitudes. The queen goes there almost every
summer, in order to escape, for a time, from the
thraldom of state ceremony, and the pomp and

parade of royal life, and live in peace among the mountain solitudes.

The soldier pointed to the coping of the wall, where the figure of a crown was cut in the stone, and the letters " V. R." by the side of it. This inscription was a memorial of the queen's having stood at this spot to view and admire the beauty of the scenery.

After Mr. George and the boys had seen all that they wished of the castle, Mr. George gave the soldier a shilling, and they went out as they had gone in, under the great archway. They passed across the esplanade, and then came to a small, level piece of ground, with a high rock beyond it, overlooking it. The level place was an ancient tilting ground; that is, a ground where, in ancient times, they used to have tilts and tournaments, for the amusement of the people of the palace, and of the guests who came to visit them. The ladies used to stand on the top of the rock to witness the tournaments. There was a large, flat area there, with room enough upon it for twenty or thirty ladies to stand and see. The rock was called the Lady's Rock. The tournaments and tiltings have long since ceased, but it retains the name of the Lady's Rock to the present day.

" Let us go up on it," said Rollo, " and see where the ladies stood."

There were a number of children playing about these grounds, and several of them were upon the top of the Lady's Rock. They looked ragged and poor. Rollo and Waldron climbed up to the place. The path was steep and rugged. When they reached the top they looked down to the level area where the tournaments were held.

"I don't think the place is big enough for a tournament," said Rollo.

"What is a tournament?" asked Waldron.

"A sort of sham fight of horsemen," said Rollo, "that they used to have in old times, when they wore steel armor, and fought with spears and lances. They used to ride against each other with blunt spears, and see who could knock the other one off his horse. What are you laughing at, uncle George?"

Rollo perceived that Mr. George was smiling at his very unromantic mode of describing a tournament. "Is not that what they used to do at the tournaments?"

"Yes," said Mr. George, "that is a pretty fair account of it, on the whole. And now, boys," he continued, "I have got a plan of having a picnic to-day, out under the castle walls here, instead of going to the hotel for dinner; and we will go and find a good place for it."

The boys said that they would like this plan

very much. " But then," said they, " we have not
got any thing to eat."

Mr. George then explained to them that the
plan which he had formed, was for them to go
down into the town, and buy something at the
shops for a picnic dinner, while he remained on
the rocks, or on some seat on the side of the Castle Hill, writing in his journal.

" Well," said Waldron, " we will do that. But
what shall we buy ? "

" Whatever you please," said Mr. George.
" Walk along through the street, and look in at
the shop windows, and whenever you see any
thing that you think we shall like, buy it."

" Well," said Rollo, " we will. But how much
shall we spend ? "

" As much as you think it best," said Mr.
George. " I leave every thing to you. You see,
our dinner at the hotel would not be less than
seven shillings, and that we shall save ; so that
if you don't spend more than seven shillings you
will be safe."

The boys were sure that they could procure
very abundant supplies for less money than that ;
and they very readily undertook the commission.
They accordingly left Mr. George at a seat near
one of the walks on the side of Castle Hill, where,
as he said, he could look right down on the famous

field of Bannockburn, and they then began to run down the walk, on the way towards the hotel.

They first went to the hotel to get a knapsack. They told the waiter there that they should not be at home to dinner. They then walked along the street, looking out for eatables. They soon found various shop windows where such things were displayed, and in the course of a quarter of an hour they had laid in an abundant supply. They bought some small, flat cakes of bread at one place, and a veal and ham pie at another, and two oranges apiece at another, and a bottle of milk at another, and finally, for dessert, they got a pound of raisins and almonds mixed together, which they chanced to see in a fruiterer's window. The cost of the whole, the boys found, when they came to foot up the account, was only two shillings and fourpence.

With these supplies the boys went up the hill again ; not through the street, but by the walk under the trees, outside the town wall. They found Mr. George in the seat where they had left him. He had just finished his writing. He was very much pleased with the purchases that the boys had made, and they all sat down together on the stone seat, and ate their dinner with excellent appetites.*

* See Frontispiece.

While they were eating the raisins and almonds Mr. George pointed down to a beautiful
field, yellow with buttercups, and said,—

"There, boys, do you see that field ?"

The boys said they did.

"It is the field of Bannockburn. Look at it,
and remember it well. When you are five years
older, and read the history of Scotland, you will
take great pleasure in thinking of the day when
you looked down from Stirling Castle on the
field of Bannockburn.'

CHAPTER XI.

LOCH LEVEN.

" AND where are we going next, uncle George?"
said Rollo, as they were all coming home to the
hotel, from their last walk up to the castle.

" I am going to Kinross," said Mr. George.

" What is there at Kinross ? " asked Rollo.

" There is a lake," said Mr. George, " and in
the lake is an island, and on the island are the
ruins of an old castle, and in the castle Mary,
Queen of Scots, was imprisoned."

" Yes," said Waldron, " I have heard of Mary,
Queen of Scots, but I do not know much about
her."

Waldron, it must be confessed, was not much
of a scholar. He had read very little, either of
history or of any thing else.

" What was she remarkable for ? " he asked.

" In the first place," said Mr. George, " she
was very beautiful, and she was also very lovely."

" That is the same thing ; is it not ? " said Rollo.

" No, not by any means," said Mr. George.

"There are many beautiful girls that are not lovely, and there are many lovely girls that are not particularly beautiful."

"You mean lovely in character, I suppose," said Rollo.

"No," said Mr. George, "I mean lovely in looks. There is a great difference, *I* think, between loveliness and beauty, in *looks*."

"I think so, too," said Waldron.

"Now, Mary, Queen of Scots," continued Mr. George, "was beautiful, and she was also very lovely ; and while she lived she charmed and fascinated almost every body who knew her.

"Then, besides," continued Mr. George, "her life was an exceedingly romantic one. She met with an extraordinary number of most remarkable adventures. She was sent to France, when she was a little child, to be educated. There were four little girls of her own age sent with her, to be her playmates there, and they were all named Mary. She called them her four Marys.

"She grew up to be a young lady in France, and married the king's son, and she lived there for a time in great prosperity and splendor. At last her husband died, and her enemies came into power in France, and she became unhappy. Besides, there were some difficulties and troubles in

Scotland, and she was obliged to return to her native land. She was, however, very unhappy about it. She loved France very much, and the friends that she had made there, and when she came away she said that she had left half her heart behind.

"When we go to Edinburgh," continued Mr. George, "we shall go to Holyrood, and see the palace where she lived. While she was there a great many extraordinary and curious events and incidents befell her."

"Tell us about them," said Waldron.

"No," said Mr. George. "It would take me too long. You must read her history yourself. It is an exceedingly interesting story. She was accused of some great crimes, but mankind have never been able to decide whether she was guilty of them or not. Some are very sure that she was innocent, and some are equally positive that she was guilty."

"What crimes were they?" asked Waldron.

"Why, one was," said Mr. George, "that of murdering her husband. It was her second husband, one that she married after she came to Scotland. They did not live happily together. He killed one of Mary's friends, named Rizzio, and afterwards he was killed himself. The house that he was in was blown up in the night with gunpowder."

" My!" exclaimed Waldron; " I should like to
read about it."

" It is a very interesting and curious story,"
said Mr. George.

" And could not they find out who did it ? "
asked Waldron.

" Yes," said Mr. George, " they found out who
did it ; but what they could not find out was,
whether Mary herself took any part in the crime
or not.   There was no direct proof.   They could
only judge from the circumstances."

" What were the circumstances ? " asked Waldron.

" O, I could not tell you very well," said Mr.
George.   " It would take me half a day to tell
the whole story.   You must get some life of
Mary, Queen of Scots, and read it for yourself.
You will have to begin at the beginning, and
read it all carefully through, and remember all
the persons that are mentioned, and consider
their characters and motives, and then you will
be able to judge for yourself about it.   There
have been a great many histories of her life
written."

" And what about her being imprisoned in the
castle that we are going to see ? " asked Waldron.

" O, you must read and find out for yourself

Waldron advised to read the Life of Mary, Queen of Scots.

about that, too," said Mr. George. " The country got into great difficulty, and two parties were
formed, one of which was in favor of Mary, and
one was against her. Her enemies proved to be
the strongest, and so they shut her up in this castle. But she got away."

" How ? " asked Waldron.

" You will learn all about it," replied Mr.
George, " when you come to read the history of
her life. When we go to the castle you will see
the window where she climbed down into the
boat."

" Did she escape in a boat ? " asked Waldron.

" I am positively not going to tell you any
more about it," said Mr. George. " You must
find out for yourself. Your father has paid ever
so much money to send you to school, to have
you educated, so that you could read history for
yourself, and not be dependent upon any body ;
and now for me to tell it to you would be ridicu-
lous. You must go to a bookstore, and buy a
history of Mary, Queen of Scots, and begin at
the beginning, and read the whole story."

Mr. George said this in a somewhat jocose sort
of manner, and Waldron understood that his
refusing to give him more full information about
Mary, Queen of Scots, arose, not from any un-
willingness to oblige him, but only to induce

him to read the story himself, in full, which he
knew very well would be far better for him than
to receive a meagre statement of the principal
points of the narrative from another person.

" I mean to get the book," said Waldron, " as
soon as we arrive at Edinburgh. But there is
one thing I can do," he added ; " I can ask the
guide. The guide that shows us the castle will
tell me how she got away."

" Well," said Mr. George, "you can ask the
guide ; but I don't believe you will get much satisfaction in *that* way."

The next morning after this conversation took
place, Mr. George and the boys bade Stirling
farewell, and set off in the cars, on the way to
Loch Leven. After riding about an hour they
left the train at the station called Dunfermline,
where there was a ruin of an abbey, and of an
ancient royal palace of Scotland. They left their
baggage at the station, and walked through the
village till they came to the ruin. It was a very
beautiful ruin, and the party spent more than an
hour in rambling about it, and looking at the old
monuments, and the carved and sculptured windows, and arches, and cornices, all wasted and
blackened by time and decay. A part of the
ruin was still in good repair, and was used as a
church, though it was full of old sepulchral

monuments and relics. There was a woman in attendance at the door, to show the church to those who wished to see the interior of it.

After looking at these ruins as long as they wished, Mr. George and the boys went back to the station, in order to take the next train that came by, and continue their journey. They went on about an hour longer, and then they got out again at a station called Cowdenbeath, which was the place on the road that was nearest to Loch Leven, and where they had understood that there was a coach, which went to Loch Leven twice a day. The place was very quiet and still, and was in the midst of a green and pretty country, with small groups of stone cottages here and there. There were also several pretty tall chimneys scattered about the fields, with a sort of platform, and some wheels and machinery near each of them. These were the mouths of coal pits. The wheels and machinery were for hoisting up the coal.

In the yard of the station they found the Loch Leven coach. It was in the form of a very short omnibus. The coachman said that he had just come in from Loch Leven, and that he was going to set out on his return at eight. It was now about seven, so that Mr. George and the boys had an hour to walk about, and see what was to be seen.

It was a pleasant summer evening, and they
enjoyed the rambles that they took very much
indeed. They walked through several of the little hamlets, and saw the women sitting at the
doors of their cottages, with their young children
in their arms, while the older ones were running
about, here and there, at play. They went to
some of the coal pits, and saw the immense iron
levers, driven by steam, that were slowly moving
to and fro, hard at work pumping up water from
the bottom of the mine. They took quite a walk,
too, along the turnpike road, and saw a post-
chaise drive swiftly by, with a footman behind,
and a postilion in livery on one of the horses.

At last, when the hour of eight began to draw
nigh, they all went back to a little inn near the
station, where the coachman had said that he
would call for them. When the coach came Mr.
George got in, and the two boys mounted on the
top, and took their places on a high seat behind
that of the driver. They had a very pleasant
ride. The country was beautiful, and the horses
trotted so fast over the smooth, hard road, that a
continued succession of most enchanting pictures
of rural scenery was presented to the eyes of the
boys, as they rode along. The distance was not
far from ten miles, but both the boys wished that
it had been twenty.

At length they came in sight of a large village bordered by groves of trees, lying in the midst of a gentle depression of the ground, and in a few minutes more they began to get glimpses of the water. The village was Kinross, and the water was Loch Leven. Presently, in going over a gentle elevation of land, a large portion of the surface of the water came into view. Far out towards the centre of it was a small, low island, covered with trees. In the midst of the trees the boys could see the top of the ruin of a large, square tower. They asked the coachman if that was Loch Leven Castle, and he said it was.

" Uncle George," said Rollo, leaning over and calling out to his uncle inside, " there's the castle."

" Yes," said Mr. George, " I see it."

" It seems to me," said Rollo to Waldron, "that that is a very small island to build a castle upon."

" Yes," said the coachman; " but it was a great deal smaller in the days when the castle was inhabited. It was only just large enough then for the castle itself, and for the castle garden. It is a great deal larger now. The way it came to be larger was this. Some years ago the proprietor cut down the outlet of the loch four feet deeper than it was before; and that drew

off four feet of water from the whole loch, and
of course all the places where the water was
less than four feet deep were laid bare. This
enlarged the castle island a great deal, for before
the water was very shallow all around it. When
the land became dry they planted trees there,
and now the ruins are in the midst of quite a
grove."

By this time the coach began to enter the village, and very soon it stopped at the door of a
very neat and tidy-looking inn. Mr. George engaged lodgings for the night, and called for supper. The supper was served in a pleasant little
coffee room, which was fitted up in a very snug
and comfortable manner, like a back parlor in a
gentleman's house.

After supper Mr. George proposed to the boys
that they should take a walk about the village,
as it was only nine o'clock, and it would not be
dark for another hour. So they went out and
walked through the street, back and forth. The
houses were built of a sort of gray stone, and
they stood all close together in rows, one on each
side of the street, with nothing green around
them or near them. The street thus presented a
very gray, sombre, and monotonous appearance ;
very different from the animated and cheerful
aspect of American villages, with their white

houses and green blinds, and pretty yards and
gardens, enclosed with ornamental palings.   The
boys wished to go down to the shore of the loch ;
but as they did not see the water any where, Mr.
George said he thought it would be too far.   So
they went back to the inn.

The next morning, after breakfast, they set out
to go and visit the castle.   A boy went with
them from the inn to show them the way.   He
led them down the street of the village, to a
house where he said the man lived who " had the
fishing " of the loch.   It seems that the loch, in-
cluding the right to fish in it, is private property,
and that the owner of it lets the fishing to a man
in the village, and that he keeps a boat to take
visitors out to see the castle.   So they went to
the house where this man lived.   They explained
what they wanted at the door, and pretty soon a
boatman came out, and went with them to the
shore of the pond.   The way was through a wide
green field, that had been formed out of the bottom of the loch, by drawing off the water.   When
they came to the shore they found a small pier
there, with a boat fastened to it.   There was a
small boat house near the pier.   The boatman
brought some oars out of the boat house, and put
them in the boat, and then they all got in.

The morning was calm, and the loch was very
10

smooth, and the boat glided along very gently
over the water. There was a great curve in the
shore near the pier, so that for some time the
boat, though headed directly for the island, which
was in the middle of the loch, moved parallel to
the shore, and very near it. There was a smooth
and beautiful green field all the way along the
shore, which sloped down gently to the margin
of the water. Beyond this field, which was not
wide, there was a road, and beyond the road
there was a wall. Over the wall were to be seen
the trees of a great park ; and presently the boat
came opposite to the gateway, through which the
boys could see, as they sailed by, a large and
handsome stone house, or castle. The boatman
said it was not inhabited, because the owner of it
was not yet of age.

After passing the house they came, before long,
to the end of these grounds, which formed a
point projecting into the lake. There was a
small and very ancient-looking burying ground
on the point. This burying ground will be referred to hereafter ; so do not forget it.

After passing this point of land, the boat, in
her course towards the castle, came out into the
open loch — the little island on which the ruins
of the castle stand being in full view.

There was, however, yet a pretty broad sheet
of open water to pass before reaching the island.

LOCH LEVEN.

" Now we have passed Cape Race," said Waldron, " and are striking out into the open sea."

Cape Race is the southern cape of Newfound-
land, and is the last land to be seen on the American coast, in crossing the Atlantic.

After about a quarter of an hour, the boat began to approach the shores of the little island.
And now the great square tower, and the rampart wall connected with it, came plainly in
sight. There were a few very large and old
trees overhanging the ruins, and all the rest of

the island was covered with a dense grove of
young trees. The boat came up to the land, and
Mr. George and the boys stepped out of it upon
a sort of jetty, formed of stones loosely thrown
together. There was a path leading through
the grass, and among the trees, towards the ruins
of the castle.

The castle consisted, when it was entire, of a
square area enclosed in a high wall, with various
buildings along the inner side of it. The principal of these buildings was the square tower.
This was in one corner of the enclosure. At the
opposite corner of the enclosure were the ruins
of a smaller tower, hexagonal in its form. The
square tower contained the principal apartments
occupied by the family that resided in the castle.
The hexagonal one contained the rooms where
Queen Mary was imprisoned.

Then, besides these structures, there were several other buildings within the area, though they
are now gone almost entirely to ruin. There was
a chapel, for religious services and worship ; there
were ovens for baking, and a brewery for brew-
ing beer. The guide showed Mr. George and
the boys the places where these buildings stood ;
though nothing was left of them now but the
rude ranges of stone which marked the founda-
tions of them. Indeed, throughout the whole

interior of the area enclosed by the castle wall
there was nothing to be seen but stones and
heaps of rubbish, all overgrown with rank grass,
and tall wild-flowers, and overshadowed by the
wide-spreading limbs and dense foliage of several
enormous trees, that had by chance sprung up
since the castle went to ruin. It was a very
mournful spectacle.

The boys walked directly across the area, towards the hexagonal tower, in order to see the
place where Queen Mary escaped by climbing
out of the window.

Mr. George had thought that Waldron would
not succeed in obtaining any satisfactory information from the guide in respect to the circumstances of Queen Mary's escape; for, generally,
the guides who show these old places in England
and Scotland know little more than a certain les-
son, which they have learned by rote. But the
guides who show the Castle of Loch Leven seem
to me exceptions to this rule. I have visited the
place two or three times, at intervals of many
years, and the guides who have conducted me to
the spot have always been very intelligent and
well-informed young men, and have seemed to
possess a very clear and comprehensive under-
standing of the events of Queen Mary's life. At
any rate, the guide in this instance gave Wal-

dron and Rollo a very good account of the
escape; separating in his narrative, in a very
discriminating manner, those things which are
known, on good historical evidence, to be true,
from those which rest only on the authority of
traditionary legends. He gave his account, too,
in a very gentle tone of voice, and with a Scotch
accent, which seemed so appropriate to the place
and to the occasion that it imparted to his conversation a peculiar charm.

"The country was divided in those days," said
he, "and some of the nobles were for the poor
queen, and some were against her. The owner
of this castle was Lady Douglass, and she was
against her; and so they sent Mary here, for Lady
Douglass to keep her safely, while they arranged
a new government.

"But she made her escape by this window,
which I will show ye."

So saying, the guide led the way up two or
three old, time-worn, and dilapidated steps, into
the hexagonal tower. The tower was small —
being, apparently, not more than twelve feet di-
ameter within. The floors, except the lower one,
and also the roof, were entirely gone, so that as
soon as you entered you could look up to the sky.

The walls were very thick, so that there was
room, not only for deep fireplaces, but also for

closets and for a staircase, in them. You could
see the openings for these closets, and also
various loopholes and windows, at different
heights. The top of the wall was all broken
away, and so were the sills of the windows; and
little tufts of grass and of wall flowers were to
be seen, here and there, growing out of clefts
and crevices. There were also rows of small
square holes to be seen, at different heights,
where the ends of the timbers had been inserted,
to form the floors of the several stories.

"This was the window where she is supposed
to have got out," said the guide.

So saying, he pointed to a large opening in
the wall, on the outer side, where there had once,
evidently, been a window.

The boys went to the place, and looked out.
They saw beneath the window a smooth, green
lawn, with the young trees which had been
planted growing luxuriantly upon it.

"I suppose," said Mr. George, "that before
the lake was lowered the water came up close
under the window."

"Yes, sir," said the guide; "and if you stand
upon the sill, and look down, you will see a
course of projecting stone at the foot of the wall,
which was laid to meet the wash of the water."

"Let me see," said Waldron, eagerly.

So saying, Waldron advanced by the side of Mr. George, and looked down. By leaning over pretty far he could see the course of stone very distinctly that the guide had referred to.

"Who brought the boat here for Mary to go away in?" asked Waldron.

"Young Douglass," said the guide, "Lady Douglass's son. He was a young lad, only eighteen years old. His mother was Queen Mary's enemy; but *he* pitied her, and became her friend, and he devised this way to assist her to escape. There was a plan devised before this, by his brother. His name was George Douglass. The one who came in the boat was William. George's plan was for Mary to go on shore in the disguise of a laundress. The laundress came over to the island from the shore in a boat, to bring the linen; and while she was in Mary's room Mary exchanged clothes with her, and attempted to go on shore in the boat with the empty basket. But the boatmen happened to notice her hand, which was very delicate and white, and they knew that such a hand as that could never belong to a real laundress. So they made her lift up her veil, and thus she was discovered."

"That was very curious," said Waldron.

"It is supposed," said the guide, "that this

floor, where we stand, was Mary's drawing room, and the floor above was her bed chamber. The staircase where she went up is *there*, in the wall."

" Let's go up," said Rollo.

So Rollo and Waldron went up the stairway. It was very narrow, and rather steep, and the steps were much worn away. When the boys reached the top they came to an opening, through which they could look down to where Mr. George and the guide were standing below ; though, of course, they could not go out ; for the floor in the second story was entirely gone.

" There was a room above the bed chamber," said the guide, " as we see by the windows and the fireplace, but there was no stairway to it from Queen Mary's apartments. The only access to it was through that door, which leads in from the top of the rampart wall. And there is another room below, and partly under ground. That is the room where Walter Scott represents the false keys to have been forged."

" What false keys ? " asked Waldron.

" Why, the story is," said the guide, " that young Douglass had false keys made, to resemble the true ones as nearly as possible, so as to deceive his mother. He then contrived to get the true ones away from his mother, and put the false ones in their place. I will show you where

he did this, and explain how he did it, when we
go into the square tower."

" Let us go now," said Waldron.

So they all went across the court yard, and
approached the square tower. The guide explained to the boys that formerly the entrance
was in the second story, through an opening in
the wall, which he showed them. The way to
get up to this opening was by a step ladder,
which could be let down or drawn up by the people within, by means of chains coming down from
a window above. The step ladder was, of course,
entirely gone ; but deep grooves were to be seen
in the sill of the upper window, which had been
worn by the chains in letting down and drawing
up the ladder.

To accommodate modern visitors a flight of
loose stone steps had been laid outside the square
tower, leading to a window in the lower story
of it. Mr. George and the boys ascended these
steps and went in. The lower room was the
kitchen, and they were all much interested and
amused in looking at the very strange and curious fixtures and contrivances which remained
there — the memorials of the domestic usages of
those ancient times.

In a corner of the room was a flight of steps,
built in the thickness of the wall, leading to the

Sir Walter Scott's account of William Douglass's plan.

story above. This was the dining room and parlor of the castle.

"It was here," said the guide, "according to the story of Walter Scott, that Douglass contrived to get possession of the castle keys. There was a window on one side of the room, from which there was a view, across the water of the lake, of the burying ground already mentioned. Lady Douglass, like almost every body else in those times, was somewhat superstitious, and William arranged it with a page that he was to pretend to see what was called a corpse light, moving about in the burying ground; and while his mother went to see, he shifted the keys which she had left upon the table, taking the true ones himself, and leaving the false ones in their place.

"That is the story which Sir Walter Scott relates," said the guide; "but I am not sure that there is any historical authority for it."

"And what became of Queen Mary, after she escaped in the boat?" asked Waldron.

"O, there were several of her friends," said the guide, "waiting for her on the shore of the loch where she was to land, and they hurried her away on horseback to a castle in the south of Scotland, and there they gathered an army for her, to defend her rights."

After this the boys looked down through a

trap door, which led to a dark dungeon, where it is supposed that prisoners were sometimes confined. They rambled about the ruins for some time longer, and then they returned to the boat, and came back to the shore. When they arrived at the pier they paid the boatman his customary fee, which was about a dollar and a quarter, and then began to walk up towards the inn.

" Well, boys," said Mr. George, " how did you like it ? "

" Very much indeed," said Waldron. " It is the best old castle I ever saw."

" You will like the Palace of Holyrood better, I think," said Mr. George.

" Where is that ? " asked Rollo.

" At Edinburgh," said Mr. George. " It is the place where Mary lived. We shall see the little room there where they murdered her poor secretary, David Rizzio."

" What did they murder him for ? " asked Waldron.

" O, you will see when you come to read the history," said Mr. George. " It is a very curious story."

CHAPTER XII.

EDINBURGH.

FROM Loch Leven Castle our party returned in the coach to the railway station, and thence proceeded to Edinburgh. They crossed the Frith of Forth by a ferry, at a place where it was about five miles wide.

Edinburgh is considered one of the most remarkable cities in the world, in respect to the picturesqueness of its situation. It stands upon and among a very extraordinary group of steep hills and deep valleys. A part of it is very ancient, and another part is quite modern, so that in describing it, it is often said that it consists of the old town and the new town. But it seems to me that a more obvious distinction would be, to divide it into the upper town and the lower town ; for there are almost literally two towns, one upon the top of the other. The upper town is built on the hills. The lower one lies in the valleys. The streets of the upper town are connected by bridges ; and when you stand upon one of these bridges, and look down, you see a street instead of a river below, with ranges of strange and antique-looking buildings on each side, for banks, and a current of men, women, and children flowing along, instead of water.

The different portions of the lower town, on the other hand, are connected by tunnels and arched passage ways under the bridges above described ; and then there are flights of steps, and steep winding or zigzag paths, leading up and down between the lower streets and the upper, in the most surprising manner.

There are twenty places, more or less, in the town, where you have two streets crossing each other at right angles, one fifty feet below the other, with an immense traffic of horses, carriages, carts, and foot passengers, going to and fro in both of them. You come upon these places sometimes very unexpectedly. You are walking along on the pavement of a crowded street, when you come suddenly upon the break, or interruption in the line of building on each side. The space is occupied by a parapet, or by a high iron balustrade. You stop to look over, expecting to see a river or a canal ; instead of which, you find yourself looking down into the chimneys of four-story houses bordering another street below you, which is so far down that the people walking in it, and the children playing on the sidewalk, look like pygmies.

At one place, in looking over the parapet of such a bridge, you see a vast market, with carts filled with vegetables standing all around it. At another, you behold a great railway station, with crowds of passengers on the platforms, and trains of cars coming and going ; at another, a range of beautiful gardens and pleasure grounds, with ladies and gentlemen walking in them, or sitting on seats under the trees, and children trundling their hoops, or rolling their balls, over the smooth gravel walks.

Sometimes a street of the upper town, running along on the crest or side of a hill, lies *parallel* with one in the lower town, that extends below it in the valley. In this case the block of houses that comes between will be very high indeed on the side towards the lower street ; so that you see buildings sometimes eight or ten stories high at one front, and only four or five on the other. These structures consist, in fact, of two houses, one on top of the other ; the entrances to the lower house being from one of the streets of the lower town, and those leading to the one on the top being from a street in the upper town.

The reason why Edinburgh was built in this extraordinary position was, because it had its

origin in a castle on a rock. This rock, with the
castle that crowns the summit of it, rears its lofty
head now in the very centre of the town, with
deep valleys all around it. This rock, or rather
rocky hill, — for it is nearly a mile in circumfer-
ence, — is very steep on all sides but one. On that
side there is a gradual slope, a mile or more in
length, leading down to the level country. A
great many centuries ago the military chieftains
of those days built the castle on the hill. About
the same time the monks built a monastery on
the level ground at the foot of the long slope
leading down from the castle. The rocky hill
was an excellent place for the castle, for there
was a hundred feet of almost perpendicular precipice on all sides but one, and on that side there
was a convenient slope for the people who lived
in the castle to go up and down ; and thus, by
fortifying this side, and making slight walls on
all the other sides, the whole place would be very
secure. The level ground below, too, was a very
good place for the monastery or abbey ; for it
was easily accessible from all the country around,
and was, moreover, in the midst of a region of
fertile land, easy for the lay brethren to till.
There was no necessity that the abbey should be
in a fortified place, for such establishments were

considered sacred in those days, and even in the
most furious wars they were seldom molested.

In process of time a palace was built by the
side of the abbey. This palace and a part of
the ruins of the abbey still remain. Of course,
when the palace was built, a town would gradually grow up near it. Many noblemen of the
realm came and built houses along the street
which led from the palace up to the castle — now
called High Street. The fronts of these houses
were on the street, and the gardens behind them
extended down the slopes of the ridge on both
sides, into the deep valleys that bordered them.
Little lanes were left between these houses, leading down the slopes; but they were closed at the
bottom by a wall, which was built along at the
foot of the descent on each side, and formed the
enclosure of the town.

In process of time the town extended down
into these valleys, and then to the other hills beyond them. Then bridges were built here and
there across the valleys, to lead from one hill to
another, and tunnels and other subterranean pas-
sages were made, to connect one valley with
another, until, finally, the town assumed the very
extraordinary appearance which it now presents
to view. Besides the hills within the town, there
are some very large and high ones just beyond

11

the limits of it. One of these is called Arthur's
Seat, and is quite a little mountain. The path
leading to the top of it runs along upon the crest
of a remarkable range of precipices, called Salis-
bury Crags. These precipices face towards the
town, and together with the lofty summit of Arthur's Seat, which rises immediately behind them,
form a very conspicuous object from a great
many points of view in and around the town.

Unfortunately, however, none of this exceedingly picturesque scenery could be seen to advan-
tage by our party, on the day that they arrived
in Edinburgh, on account of the rain. All that
they knew was, that they came into the town by
a tunnel, and when they left the train at the station they were at the bottom of so deep a valley
that they had to ascend to the third story before
they could get out, and then they had to go up a
hill to get to the street in which the hotel was
situated.

The name of this street was Prince's Street.
It lay along the margin of one of the Edinburgh
hills, overlooking a long valley, which extended
between it and Castle Hill, on which the town
was first built. There were no houses in this
street on the side towards the valley, but there
were several bridges leading across the valley, as
if it had been a river. Beyond the valley were

to be seen the backs of the houses in High Street, which looked like a range of cliffs, divided by vertical chasms and seams, and blackened by time. At one end of the hill was the castle rock, crowned with the towers, and bastions, and battlemented walls of the ancient fortress.

The boys went directly to their rooms when they arrived at the hotel, and while Mr. George was unstrapping and opening his valise, Waldron and Rollo went to look out at the window, to see what they could see.

"Well, boys," said Mr. George, "how does it look ? "

"It looks rainy," said Rollo. "But we can see something."

"What can you see ? " asked Mr. George.

"We can see the castle on the hill," said Rollo. "At least, I suppose it is the castle. It is right before us, across the valley, with a precipice of rocks all around it, on every side but one. There is a zigzag wall running round on the top of the precipices, close to the brink of them. If a man could climb up the rocks he could not get in, after all."

"And what is there inside the wall ? " asked Mr. George.

"O, there are ever so many buildings," said

Rollo — " great stone forts, and barracks, and bastions, rising up one above another, and watch towers on the angles of the walls. I can see one, two, three watch towers. I should like to be in one of them. I could look over the whole city, and all the country around.

" I can see some portholes, with guns pointing out, — and — O, and now I see a monstrous great gun, looking over this way, from one of the highest platforms. I believe it is a gun."

"I suppose it must be Mons Meg," said Mr. George.

" Mons Meg ? " repeated Rollo. " I'll get a glass and see."

" Yes," said Mr. George. " There is a very famous old gun in Edinburgh Castle, named Mons Meg. I think it may be that."

" I can't see very plain," said Rollo, " the air is so thick with the rain ; but it is a monstrous gun."

Just at this time the waiter came into the room to ask the party if they would have any thing to eat.

" Yes," said Mr. George, " we will. Go down with the waiter, boys, and see what there is, and order a good supper. I will come down in fifteen minutes."

So the boys went down, and in fifteen minutes

Mr. George followed. He found the supper table ready in a corner of the coffee room, and Rollo sitting by it alone.

"Where is Waldron?" asked Mr. George.

"He's gone to the circulating library," said Rollo.

"The circulating library?" repeated Mr. George.

"He has gone to get a book about the history of Scotland," said Rollo. "We have been reading in the guide book about the castle, and Waldron says he wants to know something more about the kings, and the battles they fought."

"How does he know there is any circulating library?" asked Mr. George.

"He asked the waiter," said Rollo, "and the waiter told him where there was one. He said he would try to be back before the supper was ready, and that we must not wait for him if he did not come."

"He ought to have asked me if I was willing that he should go," said Mr. George.

In a few minutes Waldron came in with two pretty big books under his arm. They were covered with paper, in the manner usual with the books of circulating libraries. Waldron advanced to the supper table, and laid the books down upon it with an air of great satisfaction.

"Then you found a circulating library," said Mr. George.

"Yes, sir," said Waldron, "and I have got two volumes of the history of the great men of Scotland."

"What did you get two volumes for?" asked Mr. George.

"One for Rollo and one for me," said Waldron. "They are for us to read this evening, because it rains."

"Well," said Mr. George, after a moment's pause. "I am very glad to find that you take an interest in reading about Scotland; but you ought to have asked me, before you went away to get books from a circulating library."

Waldron paused a moment on hearing this remark, and his countenance assumed a very serious expression.

"So I ought," said he. "I did not think of that. And now, if you think I had better, I will go and carry them right back."

"No," said Mr. George, "I don't wish you to carry them back. But I should not have thought they would have intrusted such books to you — a perfect stranger — and a boy besides."

"I made a deposit," said Waldron.

Just at this time the waiter brought the supper

to the table, and the party, being all hungry, set themselves to the work of eating it.

"You see," said Waldron, when they had nearly finished their supper, "I thought we should want something to do this evening; it rains, and we can't go out."

"What time in the evening do you suppose it is?" asked Mr. George.

"Why, it is not near dark yet," said Waldron.

"True," said Mr. George; "but it is almost ten o'clock."

O Mr. George!" exclaimed Waldron.

"It is half past nine, at any rate," said Mr. George.

The boys were greatly surprised at hearing this. They were very slow in learning to keep in mind how late the sun goes down in the middle of June in these extreme northern latitudes.

However, on this occasion it was dark earlier than usual, on account of the clouds and the rain; and the waiter came to light the gas over the table where our party were at supper, before they finished their meal, although it was only a little more than half past nine. This made it very bright and cheerful in the corner, and Mr. George proposed that they should all stay there one hour. "I will write," said he, "and you may read in your books. We will stay here till half past ten, and

then, after you have gone to bed, you can talk
yourselves to sleep by telling each other what
you have read about in your books."

This plan was carried into effect. Mr. George
wrote, and the boys read, by the light of the gas
for an hour. Then Mr. George put away his
papers, and said it was time to go to bed. When
the boys went to their bedroom they found two
narrow beds in it, one in each corner of the
room. Waldron took one of them, and Rollo the
other. When both the boys were in bed they
commenced conversation in respect to what they
had been reading.

" Come, Waldron," said Rollo, " tell me what
you have been reading about."

" No," said Waldron, " you must begin."

" Well," said Rollo, " I read about King James
the First. There have been a good many King
Jameses in Scotland."

" Yes," said Waldron, " six."

" This was King James the First. He was a
bad king. He oppressed his people, and they
determined to kill him. So they banded together
and made a plot. They were going to kill him
in a monastery where he stopped on a journey.

" He was going over a river just before he
came to the monastery, and a woman, who pretended to be a prophetess, called out to him as

he went by towards the bank of the river, and told him to beware, for if he crossed that river he would certainly be killed. The king was very superstitious; so he sent one of his men back to ask the woman what she meant. The man came to him again very soon, and said that it was nothing but an old drunken woman raving, and that he must not mind her. So the king went on.

" He crossed the water, and went to the monastery. The conspirators were there before him. The leader of them was a man named Graham. He had three hundred Highlanders with him. They were all concealed in the neighborhood of the monastery. They were going to break into the king's room in the monastery, at night, and kill him. They found out the room where he was going to sleep, and they took off the bolts from the doors, so as to keep them from fastening them.

" The woman that had met the king on the way followed him to the monastery, and wanted to see the king. They told her she could not see him. She said she *must* see him. They told her that at any rate she could not see him then — he was tired with his journey. She must go away, they said, and come the next day. So she went away; but she told them they would all be sorry for not letting her in."

" Do you suppose she really knew," asked
Waldron, " that they were going to kill the
king ? "

" I don't know," said Rollo. " At any rate,
she seemed very much in earnest about warning
him."

" Well ; go on with the story," said Waldron.

" Why, the conspirators broke into the room
that night just as the king was going to bed. He
was sitting near the fire, in his gown and slip-
pers, talking with the queen and the other ladies
that were there, when, all at once, he heard a
terrible noise at the doors of the monastery. It
was the conspirators trying to get in."

" Why did not they come right in," asked
Waldron, " if the doors were not fastened ? "

" Why, I suppose there were guards, or something, outside, that tried to prevent them. At
any rate, the king heard a frightful noise, like
clattering and jingling of armor, and of men trying to get in. He and the women who were
there ran to the door and tried to fasten it ;· but
the bolts and bars were gone. So the king told
them to hold the door with all their strength, till
he could find something to fasten it with. The
king went to the window, and tried to tear off
an iron stanchion there was there, but he could
not. Then he saw a trap door in the floor, which

led down to a kind of dark dungeon. So he took
the tongs and pried up the door, and jumped
down.

"By the time that he got down, and the door
was shut over him, the conspirators came in, and
began to look all about for him ; but they could
not find him. I suppose they did not see the
trap door. Or, perhaps, the women had covered
it over with something."

"Well, and what did they do ?" asked Waldron.

"Why, they were dreadfully angry because
they could not find the king, and some of them
were going to kill the queen ; but the rest would
not let them. But there was one of the women
that got her arm broken."

"How ?" asked Waldron.

"She did it somehow or other holding the
door. I suppose she got it wedged in some way.
She was a countess.

"After a while," continued Rollo, "the men
went away to look in some of the other rooms of
the monastery, and see if they could not find the
king there. As soon as they were gone the king
wanted to get out of the dungeon. The women
opened the trap door, but he could not reach up
high enough to get out. So he told them to go

and get some sheets and let them down, for ropes
to pull him up by.

"They brought the sheets, and while they were
letting them down, and trying to get the king
out, one of the ladies fell down herself into the
hole. So there were two to get up; and while
the others were trying to get them up, the conspirators came in again."

"Hoh!" said Waldron.

"One of them had a torch," said Rollo, con-
tinuing his narrative. "He brought the torch
and held it down the trap door, and presently he
caught sight of the king. So he called out to the
other conspirators that he had found him, and
they all came round the place, with their swords,
and daggers, and knives in their hands.

"One of them let himself down into the dungeon. He had a great knife in his hand for a
dagger. But the king seized him the instant he
came down, got his knife away from him, and
pinned him to the ground. The king was a very
strong man. Immediately another man came
down, and the king seized him, and held him
down in the same way. Next Graham himself
came with a sword. He stabbed the king with
his sword, and so disabled him. The king then
began to beg for his life, and Graham did not
seem to like to strike him again. But the other

conspirators, who were looking down through the trap door, said if he did not do it they would kill *him*. So at last he stabbed the king again, and killed him."

When Rollo had finished the story he paused, expecting that Waldron would say something in relation to it.

" Is that all ? " said Waldron, after waiting a moment. He spoke, however, in a very sleepy tone of voice.

" Yes," said Rollo, " that is all. Now tell me your story."

Waldron began; but he seemed very sleepy, and he had advanced only a very little way before his words began to grow incoherent and faltering, and very soon Rollo perceived that he was going to sleep. Indeed, Rollo himself was beginning to feel sleepy, too ; so he said, —

" No matter, Waldron. You can tell me your story to-morrow."

In five minutes from that time both the boys were fast asleep.

174   ROLLO IN SCOTLAND.

The Palace of Holyrood.   Mary the last Scotch sovereign.

CHAPTER XIII.

THE PALACE OF HOLYROOD.

WHILE Mr. George and the boys were in Edinburgh, they went one day to visit the Palace of Holyrood, and they were extremely interested in what they saw there. This palace stands, as has already been stated, on a plain, not far from the foot of a long slope which leads up to the castle.

As long as Scotland remained an independent kingdom, the Palace of Holyrood was the principal residence of the royal family. Queen Mary was the last of the Scottish sovereigns — that is, she was the last that reigned over Scotland alone — for her son, James VI., succeeded to the throne of England, as well as to that of Scotland. The reason of this was, that the English branch of the royal line failed, and he was the next heir. So he became James the First of England, while he still remained James the Sixth of Scotland. And from this time forward the kings of England and Scotland were one.

Mary, therefore, was the last of the exclusively

Scottish line. She lived at Holyrood as long as she was allowed to live any where in peace; and on account of certain very peculiar circumstances which occurred just before the time that she left the palace, her rooms were never occupied after she left them, but have remained to this day in the same state, and with almost the same furniture in them as at the hour when she went away. These rooms are called Queen Mary's rooms, and almost every body who visits Scotland goes to see them.

The reason why the rooms which Mary occupied in the Palace of Holyrood were left as they were, and never occupied by any other person after Mary went away, was principally that a dreadful murder was committed there just before Mary quitted them. This, of course, connected very gloomy associations with the palace; and while great numbers of persons were eager to go and see the place where the man was killed, few would be willing to live there. The consequence has been, that the apartments have been vacant of occupants ever since, though they are filled all the time with a perpetually flowing stream of visitors. The circumstances of the murder were very extraordinary. Mr. George explained the case briefly to the boys during their visit to the palace, as we shall presently see.

On leaving the hotel they went for a little way along Prince's Street. On one side of the street there was a row of stores, hotels, and other such buildings, as in Broadway, in New York. On the other side extended the long and deep valley which lies between Prince's Street and Castle Hill. The valley was crossed by various bridges, and beyond it were to·be seen the backs of the lofty houses of High Street, rising tier above tier to a great height, looking, as has already been said, like a range of stupendous cliffs, lifting their crests to the sky.

There were scarcely any buildings on the valley side of the street, except one or two edifices of an ornamental or public character. One of these was the celebrated monument to Sir Walter Scott.

The party paused a short time before this monument, and then went on. They passed by one or two bridges that led across the valley, and also, at one place, a broad flight of steps, that went down, with many turnings, from landing to landing, to the railway station in the valley. At last they came to the bridge where they were to cross the valley. They stopped on the middle of the bridge, to look down. They saw streets far below them, and a market, and trains of railway carriages coming and going, and be-

12   SCOTT'S MONUMENT.

yond, at some distance, an extensive range of
pleasure grounds, with ladies and gentlemen rambling about them, and groups of children playing.
These pleasure grounds extended some way up
the slope of the Castle Hill. Indeed, the upper
walks lay close along under the foot of the
precipices on which the castle walls were built
above.

After passing the bridge, Mr. George and the
boys went on, until, at length, they came to High
Street ; which is the great central street of ancient Edinburgh, leading from the palace and
abbey on the plain up to the castle on the hill.
There, if they had turned to the right, they would
have gone up to the castle ; but they turned to
the left, and so descended towards the palace, on
the plain.

At length they reached the foot of the descent,
and then, at a turn in the street, the palace came
suddenly into view.

There was a broad paved area in front of it.
In the centre of the building was a large arched
doorway, with a sentry box on each side. At
each of these sentry boxes stood a soldier on
guard. All the royal palaces of England are
guarded thus. There was a cab, that had brought
a company of visitors to see the castle, standing
near the centre of the square, by a great statue

that was there.   Another cab drove up just at
the time that Mr. George arrived, and a party
of visitors got out of it.   All the new comers
went in under the archway together.   The soldiers paid no attention to them whatever.

The arched passage way led into a square
court, with a piazza extending all around it.   The
visitors turned to the left, and walked along
under the piazza till they came to the corner,
where there was a little office, and a man at the
window of it to give them tickets.   They paid
sixpence apiece for their tickets.

After getting their tickets they walked on under the piazza a little way farther, till at length
they came to a door, and a broad stone staircase,
leading up into the palace, and they all went in
and began to ascend the stairs.

At the head of the stairs they passed through
a wide door, which led into a room where they
saw visitors, that had gone in before them, walking about.   They were met at the door by a well-
dressed man, who received them politely, and
asked them to walk in.

"This, gentlemen," said he, "was Lord Darnley's audience chamber.   That," he continued,
pointing through an open door at the side, "was
his bedroom; and there," pointing to another

small door on the other side, " was the passage
way leading up to Queen Mary's apartments."

Having said this, the attendant turned away
to answer some questions asked him by the other
visitors, leaving Mr. George and the boys, for
the moment, to look about the rooms by themselves.

The rooms were large, but the interior finish-
ing of them was very plain. The walls were
hung with antique-looking pictures. The furniture, too, looked very ancient and venerable.

" Who was Lord Darnley ? " asked Waldron.

" He was Queen Mary's husband," replied Mr.
George.

" Then he was the king, I suppose," said Waldron.

"No," replied Mr. George, "not at all. A king
is one who inherits the throne in his own right.
When the throne descends to a woman, she is the
queen ; but if she marries, her husband does not
become king."

" What is he then ? " said Waldron.

" Nothing but the queen's husband," said Mr.
George.

" Hoh ! " exclaimed Waldron, in a tone of con-
tempt.

" He does not acquire any share of the queen's
power," continued Mr. George, " because he mar-

ries her. She is the sovereign alone afterwards just as much as before."

" And so I suppose," said Rollo, " that when a king marries, the lady that he marries does not become a queen."

" Yes," said Mr. George, " the rule does not seem to work both ways. A lady who marries a king is always called a queen ; though, after all, she acquires no share of the royal power. She is a queen in name only. But let us hear what this man is explaining to the visitors about the paintings and the furniture."

So they advanced to the part of the room where the attendant was standing, with two or three ladies and gentlemen, who were looking at one of the old pictures that were hanging on the wall. It was a picture of Queen Mary when she was fifteen years old. The dress was very quaint and queer, and the picture seemed a good deal faded; but the face wore a very sweet and charming expression.

" I think she was a very pretty girl," whispered Waldron in Rollo's ear.

" She was in France at that time," said the attendant, " and the picture, if it is an original, must have been painted there, and she must have brought it with her to Scotland, on her return from that country. She brought a great deal

with her on her return. There were several vessel loads of furniture, paintings, &c. The tapestry
in the bedroom was brought. It was wrought at
the Gobelins."

Mr. George went into the bedroom, to look at
the tapestry. Two sides of the room were hung
with it.

"It looks like a carpet hung on the walls,"
said Waldron.

"Yes," said Mr. George; "a richly embroidered
carpet."

The figures on the tapestry consisted of groups
of horsemen, elegantly equipped and caparisoned.
The horses were prancing about in a very spirited
manner. The whole work looked very dingy,
and the colors were very much faded; but it was
evident that it must have been very splendid in
its day.

After looking at the tapestry, and at the various articles of quaint and queer old furniture in
this room, the company followed the attendant
into another apartment.

"This," said he, "is the room where Lord
Darnley, Ruthven, and the rest, held their con-
sultation and formed their plans for the murder
of Rizzio; and *there* is the door leading to the
private stairway where they went up. You cannot go up that way now, but you will see where

they came out above when you go up into Queen
Mary's apartments."

"Let us go now," said Waldron.

"Well," said Mr. George, "and then we can
come into these rooms again when we come
down."

So Mr. George and the boys walked back,
through Lord Darnley's rooms, to the place where
they came in.   Here they saw that the same
broad flight of stone stairs, by which they had
come up from the court below, continued to
ascend to the upper stories.   There was a painted
inscription on a board there, too, saying, "To
Queen Mary's apartments," with a hand pointing
up the staircase.   So they knew that that was
the way they must go.

As they went up, both Rollo and Waldron
asked Mr. George to explain to them something
about the murder, so that they might know a little what they were going to see.

"Well," said Mr. George, "I will.   Let us sit
down here, and I will tell you as much as I can
tell in five minutes.   Really to understand the
whole affair, you would have to read as much as
you could read in a week.   And I assure you it
is an exceedingly interesting and entertaining
story.

"Darnley, you know, was the queen's husband.

Her first husband was the young Prince of France; but he died before Queen Mary came home. So that when she came home she was a widow; very young, and exceedingly beautiful. There is a very beautiful painting of her, I am told, in the castle."

"Let us go and see it," said Waldron.

"To-morrow," said Mr. George.

"After Queen Mary had been in Scotland some little time," continued Mr. George, "she was married again to this Lord Darnley. He was an English prince. The whole story of her first becoming acquainted with Darnley, and how the marriage was brought about, is extremely interesting; but I have not time now to tell it to you.

"After they were married they lived together for a time very happily; but at length some causes of difficulty and dissension occurred between them. Darnley was not contented to be merely the queen's husband. He wanted, also, to be king."

"I don't blame him," said Waldron.

"I should have thought," said Rollo, "that Mary would have been willing that he should be king."

"Very likely she might have been willing herself," said Mr. George, "but her people were not willing. There were a great many powerful nobles and chieftains in the kingdom, and about her

court, and they took sides, one way and the
other, and there was a great deal of trouble. It
is a long story, and I can't tell you half of it,
now. What made the matter worse was, that
Darnley, finding he could not have every thing
his own way, began to be very harsh and cruel in
his treatment of Mary. This made Mary very
unhappy, and caused her to live a great deal in
retirement, with a few near and intimate friends,
who treated her with kindness and sympathy.

" One of these was David Rizzio, the man who
was murdered. He was one of the officers of the
court. His office was private secretary. He was
a great deal older than Mary, and it seems he
was an excellent man for his office. He used to
write for the queen when it was necessary, and
perform other such duties; and as he was very
gentle and kind in his disposition, and took a
great interest in every thing that concerned the
queen, Mary became, at last, quite attached to
him, and considered him as one of her best
friends. At last Lord Darnley and his party became very jealous of him. They thought that he
had a great deal too much influence over the
queen. It was as if he were the prime minister,
they said, while they, the old nobles of the realm,
were all set aside, as if they were of no consequence at all. So they determined to kill him.

"They formed their plot in the room below, where we have just been.   It was in the evening. Mary was at supper that night in a little room in the tower up above, where we are now going. There were two or three friends with her.   The men went up the private stairway, and burst into the little supper room, and killed Rizzio on the spot."

"Let us go up and see the place," said Waldron.

So Mr. George rose, and followed by the boys, he led the way into Queen Mary's apartments.

CHAPTER XIV.

QUEEN MARY'S APARTMENTS.

BEFORE we follow Mr. George and the boys
into Queen Mary's apartments, I have one or two
other explanations to make, in addition to the
information which Mr. George communicated to
the boys on the stairs. These explanations relate
to the situation of Mary's apartments in the palace. They were in a sort of wing, which forms
the extreme left of the front of the palace. The
wing is square. It projects to the front. At the
two corners of it, in front, are two round towers,
which are surmounted above by short spires. As
there is a similar wing at the right hand end of
the front, with similar towers at the corners, the
façade of the building is marked with four towers
and four spires. The left hand portion is repre
sented in the engraving opposite.

Queen Mary's rooms are in the third story, as
seen in the engraving. The principal room is in
the square part of the wing, between the two
round towers. This was the bedroom. In the

THE CORNER TOWER OF THE PALACE OF HOLYROOD.

right hand tower, as seen in the engraving, is a small room, as large as the tower can contain, which was used by Mary as an oratory; that is, a little chapel for her private devotions. In the left hand tower was another small room, similar to the oratory, which Mary used as a private sitting room or boudoir. It is just large enough for a window and a fireplace, and for a very few persons to sit. It was in this little room that Mary was having supper, with two or three of her friends, when Darnley and his gang came up to murder Rizzio, who was one among them.

Besides Mary's bedroom, which was in the front part of the wing, between the two towers, there was another large room behind it, which also belonged to her. Darnley's apartments were very similar to the queen's, only they were in the story below. It was the custom in those days, as it is now, indeed, in high life, for the husband and wife to have separate ranges of apartments, with a private passage connecting them. In this case the private passage leading from Darnley's apartments to Mary's was in the wall. It was a narrow stairway, leading up to Mary's bedroom, and the door where it came out was very near to the door leading to the little room in the tower where Mary and her friends were taking supper on the night of Rizzio's murder.

When Mr. George and the boys reached the top of the stairs, they entered a large room, which, they were told by an attendant who was there to receive them, was Mary's audience chamber. This was the room situated back of the bedroom. The room itself, and every thing which it contained, wore a very antique and venerable appearance. The furniture was dilapidated, and the coverings of it were worn and moth-eaten. Very ancient-looking pictures were hanging on the walls. There was a large fireplace, with an immense movable iron grate in it. The grate was almost entirely worn out. The attendant who showed these rooms said that it was the oldest grate in Scotland. Still, it was not so old as the time of Mary, for it was brought into Scotland, the attendant said, by Charles II., who was Mary's great grandson.

There was a window in a very deep recess in this room. It looked out upon a green park, on the side of the palace. A very ancient-looking table stood in this recess, which, the attendant said, was brought by Mary from France. The ceiling was carved and ornamented in a very curious manner.

" And which is the door," said Waldron to the

QUEEN MARY'S BEDROOM.

13

attendant, " where Darnley and his men came in,
to murder Rizzio ? "

"That is in the next room," said the attendant.
So saying, he pointed to a door, and Mr. George
and the boys, and also two or three other visitors
whom they had found in the room when they
came in, went forward and entered the room.

" This, gentlemen and ladies," said the attendant, as they went in, " was Queen Mary's bed
chamber. The door where we are coming in was
the main or principal entrance to it.   This is the
bed and bedstead, just as they were left when
Queen Mary vacated the apartment.   That door,"
— pointing to a corner of the room diagonally
opposite to where the company had entered, —
" leads to the little boudoir * where Rizzio was
killed, and that opening in the wall by the side
of it, under the tapestry, is the place where Darnley and the other assassins came up by the private stair."

A view of the room, and of the various objects
which the attendant showing them thus pointed
out to the company, may be seen in the engraving
on the opposite page.

The bedstead is seen on the right.   It is surmounted by a heavy cornice, richly carved and

---

* A boudoir is a small private apartment, fitted up for a lady,
where she receives her intimate and confidential friends.

gilded. This cornice, and the embroidered curtains that hang from it, must have been very magnificent in their day, though now they are faded
and tattered by age. The coverings of the bed
are also greatly decayed. Only a little shred of
the blanket now remains, and that is laid upon
the bolster. The rest of it has been gradually
carried away by visitors, who for a long time
were accustomed to pull off little shreds of it to
take with them, as souvenirs of their visit. These
depredations are, however, now no longer allowed. That part of the room is now enclosed
by a cord, fastened to iron rods fixed in the floor,
so that visitors cannot approach the bed. They
are watched, too, very closely, wherever they go,
to prevent their taking any thing away. They
are not allowed to sit down in any of the chairs.

The door in the corner of the room to the left
leads into the little boudoir, or cabinet, where
Rizzio was murdered. You can see a little way
into this room, in the picture. Mr. George and
the boys went into it. There was a table on the
back side of it, with the armor, and also the
gloves, and one of the boots which Darnley wore,
lying upon it. The attendant took up a breast-
plate, which formed a part of the armor, and let
the boys lift it. It was very heavy. There was
an indentation in the front of it, where it had

been struck by a bullet. The boot, too, was pro-
digiously thick and heavy. The heel was not less
than three inches high.

There was a fireplace in this room, and over it
was an altar-piece; a sort of picture in stone,
which Mary used in her oratory, according to
the custom of the Catholics. It had been broken
to pieces and put together again. It was said
that John Knox broke it, to show his abhorrence
of Popery, but that the pieces were saved, and
it was afterwards mended.

There was also in this room a square stone,
shaped like a block, about two feet long, sawed
off from the end of a beam of timber. This was
the stone that Mary knelt upon when she was
crowned Queen of Scotland.

To the right of the door which leads to the
boudoir, under the tapestry, we see in the engraving the opening in the wall which leads to
the staircase where the conspirators came up.
The boys went in here and looked down. The
stairs were very narrow, and very dark. The
passage was closed below, so that they could
not go down. In Mary's time these stairs not
only led down to Darnley's rooms, but there was
a continuation of them down the lower story, and
thence along by a private way to Mary's place in
the chapel of the monastery, where she used to go

to attend divine service. She always went by this private way, so that nobody ever saw her go or come. They only knew that she was there by seeing the curtains drawn before the little compartment in the walls of the chapel where she was accustomed to sit.

In the deep recess of the window, seen at the left in the engraving, you will see a tall stand, with a sort of basket on the top of it. This basket contained baby linen, and was sent to Mary as a present by Queen Elizabeth of England, at the time when Mary's child was born. This was the child that afterwards became King James. He was not born here, however. He was born in the castle. His birth took place only about three months after the murder of Rizzio. The basket was a very pretty one, and it was lined with the most costly lace, only a few remnants of which are, however, remaining.

The attendant showed all these things to the visitors, and many more, which I have not time now to describe. Among the rest was a piece of embroidery set in the top of a workbox, which Mary herself worked. The top of the box was formed of a plate of glass; the embroidery was placed underneath it, so that it could be seen through the glass. It was old and faded, and the

boys did not think that it was very pretty. It
was, however, curious to see it, since Mary had
worked it with her own hands ; especially as she
did it when she was a child ; for the guide said
she embroidered it when she was only about
twelve years old.

"She was very skilful with her needle," said
the attendant. "She learned the art in France,
at the convent where she was educated. This
tapestry which hangs upon the wall was worked
by the nuns at that convent, and it is said that
Mary assisted them."

The tapestry to which the guide referred is the
same that you see in the engraving on the wall
of the room, opposite to the observer. It hung
down over the door leading to the private staircase.

Besides the bedroom and the boudoir, there
was the oratory, too ; that is, the small room cor-
responding to the boudoir, in the other round
tower. This room is not shown in the engraving,
as the opening leading into it is on the side of
the bed chamber where the spectator is supposed
to stand. It was a very small room, like a round
closet, with a window in it. It contained very
little furniture. There were two tall, carved
stands, to hold the candlesticks, on each side of
the altar, and several very ancient-looking chairs.

There was also a small and very peculiar-shaped
old mirror hanging upon the wall. It had no
frame, but the glass itself was cut into an ornamental form. This mirror was a great curiosity,
it must be confessed ; but it was past performing
any useful function, for the silver was worn off to
such an extent that it was very difficult to see
one's face in it.

After looking some time longer at Queen Mary's rooms, Mr. George and the boys went back
again to Lord Darnley's apartments below. There
they saw a picture of Queen Mary which they had
not observed before. It represented her, the man
said, in the dress she wore the day that she was
beheaded. The dress was of dark silk or velvet,
plain, but very rich. It fitted close to the form,
and came up high in the neck. The countenance
evinced the changes produced by time and grief,
but it wore the same sweet expression that
was seen in the portrait painted in her earlier
years.

"What was she beheaded for ? " asked Rollo,
while they were looking at this portrait.

"She was beheaded by the government of
Queen Elizabeth of England," replied Mr. George.
"They charged her with forming plots to dethrone
Elizabeth, and make herself Queen of England in
her place."

" And did she really form the plots ? " asked
Waldron.

" Why — yes," said Mr. George, speaking,
however, in a somewhat doubtful tone, " yes —
I suppose she did ; or, at least, her friends
and party did ; she herself consenting. You
see she was herself descended from an English king, just as Elizabeth was, and it was extremely doubtful which was the rightful heir.
Mary, and all her friends and party, claimed
that she was ; and Elizabeth, on the other hand,
insisted that *her* claim was clear and unques-
tionable."

" Which was right ? " asked Waldron.

" It is impossible to say," replied Mr. George.
" It was such a complicated case that you could
not decide it either way. The question was like
a piece of changeable silk. You could make it
look green or brown, just according to the way
you looked at it. When you come to read the
history you will see just how it was."

" Yes," said Waldron, " I mean to read all
about it."

" After the difficulties in Scotland," continued
Mr. George, " Mary's armies were driven across
the line into England, and there Mary was seized
and made prisoner. Elizabeth would have given
her her liberty if she would have renounced her

claims to the English crown — but this Mary
would not do. She was kept in prison a number
of years. At last some of her friends began to
form plots to get her out, and make her Queen
of England. She was accused of joining in these
plots, and so she was tried, convicted, and beheaded."

"And did she really join in the plots?" asked
Waldron.

"I presume so," said Mr. George. "I would
have joined in them if I had been in her place."

"So would I," said Waldron.

"Did Queen Elizabeth order her to be beheaded?" asked Rollo.

"No," said Mr. George, "not directly — or, at
least, she pretended that she did not. She appointed some judges to go and try her, on the
charge of treason, and the judges condemned her
to death. Elizabeth might have saved her if she
chose, but she did not; though afterwards, when
she heard that Mary had been executed, she pretended to be in a great rage with those who had
carried the sentence into effect, and to be deeply
grieved at her cousin's death."

"The old hag!" said Waldron.

"Why, no," said Mr. George, "I don't know
that we ought to consider her an old hag for this.
It was human nature, that is all. She may have

QUEEN ELIZABETH ON PARADE.

been sincere in her grief at Mary's death, while yet she consented to it, and even desired it, beforehand. We often wish to have a thing done, and yet are very sorry for it after it is done.

"You see," continued Mr. George, "Queen Elizabeth was a very proud and ambitious woman. She was very fond of the power, and also of the pomp and parade of royalty; and she could not endure that any one should ever question her claim to the crown."

"Well," said Waldron, "at any rate I am sorry for poor Mary."

After this, Mr. George and the boys went down the staircase where they had come up, to the court, and then proceeding along the piazza to the back corner of it, they passed through an open door that led them to the ruins of the old abbey, which stood on this spot some centuries before the palace was built. There was nothing left of this ancient edifice but the walls, and some of the pillars of the chapel. The roof was gone, and every thing was in a state of dilapidation and ruin.

There was a guide there who pointed out the place where Mary stood at the time of her marriage with Lord Darnley. The grass was grow-

ing on the spot, and above, all was open to the
sky.   Multitudes of birds were flying about, and
chirping mournfully around the naked and crum-
bling walls.

CHAPTER XV.

EDINBURGH CASTLE.

THE day after the visit which the party made to the palace, they set out from their hotel to go to the castle. As they were walking along together on the sidewalk of Prince's Street, on a sudden Waldron darted off from Rollo's side, and ran into the street, in pursuit of a cab which had just gone by. He soon overtook the cab and climbed up behind it; and then, to Mr. George's utter amazement, he reached forward along the side of the vehicle, so as to look into the window of it, and knocked on the glass. In a moment the cab stopped, the door opened, and the mystery of the case was explained to Mr. George and Rollo by seeing Waldron's father looking out at it.

"It is his father!" said Rollo.

"Yes," said Mr. George. "But that is not the proper way for a boy to stop his father, riding by in a cab, in the streets of Edinburgh."

The cab drove up to the sidewalk, and then

Mr. Kennedy got out to speak to Mr. George. He said that he had received letters from America, making it necessary for him to set sail immediately for home. He had intended, he added, to have remained two or three weeks longer in Scotland ; and in that case he should have liked very much to have continued Waldron under Mr. George's care.

"And now," he added, turning to Waldron, " which would you rather do—go home to America with me, or stay here, and travel with Mr. George ? "

Waldron looked quite perplexed at this proposal. He said that he liked very much to travel with Mr. George and Rollo, and yet he wanted very much indeed to go home.

In the course of the day various debates and consultations were held, and it was finally decided that Waldron should go home. So the accounts were settled with Mr. George, and Waldron was transferred to the hotel where his father and mother were lodging. They were to set out the next morning, in the express train for Liverpool. The preparations for the journey and the voyage kept Waldron busy all that day, so that Mr. George and Rollo went to the castle alone. But Waldron made Rollo promise that in the evening

he would come to the hotel and see him, and tell
him what he saw there.

In the evening, accordingly, Rollo went to the
hotel where Mr. Kennedy was staying. Mr.
George went with him. They went first into
Mr. Kennedy's parlor. A door was open between the parlor and one of the bedrooms, and
both rooms were full of trunks and parcels.
Every body was busy packing and arranging.
The ladies were showing each other their different purchases, as they came in from the shops;
and as soon as Mr. George entered, they began
to ask him whether he thought they would be
obliged to pay duty on this, or on that, when they
arrived in America.

Rollo asked where Waldron was, and they
said he was in his room, packing his trunk. So
Rollo went to find him.

" Ah, Rollo," said Waldron, " I am glad you
have come. I want you to sit on the top of my
trunk with me, and make it shut down."

Rollo gave Waldron the assistance he required,
and by the conjoined gravity of both the boys the
trunk was made to shut. Waldron turned the
key in an instant, and then said, —

" There! Get open again if you can. And
now, Rollo," he continued, " tell me about the
castle."

14

"Well, we had a very good time visiting it."
said Rollo. "We went over the bridge where
you and I stopped to look down to the market,
and came to High Street. But instead of turning down, as we did when we were going to
Holyrood, we turned *up ;* because, you know, the
castle is on the top of the hill."

"Yes," said Waldron, "I knew that was the
way."

"Well, we went up High Street," continued
Rollo. "The upper part of it is quite a handsome street. There were a great many large
public buildings. We passed by a great cathedral, where, they said, a woman threw a stool at
the minister, while he was preaching.

"What did she do that for?" asked Waldron.

"I don't know," said Rollo. "I suppose she
did not like his preaching. It was in the refor-
mation times. I believe he was preaching Popery,
and she was a Protestant. Her name was Jenny
Geddes. They have got the stool now."

"They have?" exclaimed Waldron.

"Yes," said Rollo, "so uncle George said.
They keep it in the Antiquarian Museum, for a
curiosity."

"When we got to the upper end of the High
Street," continued Rollo, "there was the castle
all before us. Only first there was a parade

ground for the troops ; it was all gravelled
over."

"Were there any soldiers there?" asked Waldron.

"Yes," said Rollo, "there were two or three
companies drilling and parading."

"I should like to have seen them," said Waldron.

"Yes," said Rollo, "and besides, the parade
ground was a splendid place. The lower end of
it was towards the street ; the upper end was
towards the gates and walls of the castle, and
the two sides of it were shut in by a low wall,
built on the very brink of the precipice. You
could look down over this wall into the streets
of the lower part of the town ; and then we
could see off a great way, over all the country.

"We stopped a little while to look at the
view, and then we turned round and looked at
the soldiers a little while longer, and then we
went on. Presently we came to the castle gates.
There was a sentinel on guard, and some soldiers walking to and fro on the ramparts above ;
but they did not say any thing to us, and so we
went in. There were other parties of ladies and
gentlemen going in too."

"Well," said Waldron, "what did you see
when you got in?"

" Why, we were yet only inside the walls,"
said Rollo, " and so we kept going on up a steep
road paved with stones. There were walls, and
towers, and battlements, and bastions, and soldiers walking sentry, and cannons pointed at us,
all around. Presently we came to a sort of
bridge. Here we heard some music. It seemed
down below ; so we went to the side of the bridge
and looked over. There was a little square field
below, and three men, with Scotch bagpipes, playing together. The men were dressed in uniform,
and the bagpipes were splendid-looking instru-
ments."

" Yes," said Waldron. " They were the mu-
sicians of some Highland regiment, practising."

" Well ; we went on, higher and higher," said
Rollo, " and continued going round and round,
till, at last, we came to the upper part of the
castle, where there were platforms, and cannons
upon them, pointing out over all the country
round about."

" Did you see Mons Meg ? " asked Waldron.

" Yes," said Rollo, " and we went up close to
it. But we did not touch it, for there was a notice put up that visitors must not touch the
guns.

" By and by we came into a large square
court, with buildings, that looked like barracks,

all about it. There was a sign up, with a hand
on it pointing, and the words, 'To the crown
room.' So we knew that that was the place
where we were to go. Besides, all the other
ladies and gentlemen were going there, too.

"We gave up our tickets at the door, and
went up a short flight of steps, into a little sort
of cellar."

"A little sort of cellar!" exclaimed Waldron.
He was surprised at the idea of going up stairs
into a cellar.

"Yes," said Rollo. "It was just like a cellar.
It had stone walls all around it, and was arched
overhead."

"Was it dark?" asked Waldron.

"O, no," said Rollo ; "it was lighted up splen-
didly with gas. The gas shone very bright in
between the bars of the cage, and brightened up
the crown and the jewels wonderfully."

"In the cage?" repeated Waldron ; "was
there a cage?"

"Yes," replied Rollo. "In the middle of the
room there was a great iron cage, as high as my
head, and big in proportion. The crown and
the jewels were in the cage, on cushions. They
were so far in that people could not reach them
by putting their hands through the bars. There
were a great many persons standing all around

the cage, and looking in to see the crown and the jewels."

" Were they pretty ? " asked Waldron.

"Not very," said Rollo. " I suppose the things were made of gold ; but I could not tell, from the looks of them, whether they were made of gold or brass."

" Was there any thing else ? " asked Waldron.

" Yes," said Rollo, " there was a monstrous oak chest, — iron bound, or brass bound, — where the crown and jewels were hid away for a great many years. At the time when Scotland was united to England, they put these things in this chest ; and they were left there so long that at last there was nobody that knew where they were. Finally the government began to look for them, and they looked in this old chest, and there they found them.

" While we were looking at the chest," continued Rollo, "I heard some music out in the court, and I asked uncle George to let me go out ; and he did. I was very glad I did, for the Highland regiment was paraded in the court. I stood there some time to see them exercised."

" Did they look well ? " asked Waldron.

" Beautifully," said Rollo.

After this, Rollo gave Waldron some further accounts of what he saw at the castle ; but before

EDINBURGH CASTLE. 215

Time to go home.   Good by to Waldron.

he got quite through with his descriptions Mr.
George came, and said it was time for them to go
home. So they both bade Waldron good by.
Rollo said, however, that it was not his final
good by.

"I shall come down to the station to-morrow
morning," said he, "and see you go."

Waldron was very much pleased to hear this,
and then Mr. George and Rollo went away.

CHAPTER XVI.

CONCLUSION.

MR. GEORGE and Rollo made some excursions together after this, but I have not time to give a full account of them. Among others, they went to see Linlithgow, where stands the ruin of an ancient palace, which was the one in which Queen Mary was born. Linlithgow itself is a town. Near it is a pretty little loch. The ruins stand on a smooth and beautiful lawn, between the town and the shore of the loch. The people who lived in the palace had delightful views from their windows, both of the water of the loch itself and of the opposite shores.

At this ruin people can go up by the old staircases to various rooms in the upper stories, and even to the top of the walls. The floors, wherever the floors remain, are covered with grass and weeds.

There was a very curious story about the castle. It was taken at one time by means of a load of hay. The enemy engaged a farmer who lived near, and who was accustomed to supply the people of the castle with hay, to join them in their plot. So they put some armed men on his cart, and covered them all over with hay. They also concealed some more armed men near the gateway. The gateway had what is called a portcullis; that is, a heavy iron gate suspended by chains, so as to rise and fall. Of course, when the portcullis was down, nobody could get in or out.

The people of the castle hoisted the portcullis, to let the load of hay come in, and the farmer, as soon as he had got the wagon in the middle of the gateway, stopped it there, and cut the traces, so that it could not be drawn any farther. At the same instant the men who were hid under the hay jumped out, killed the guard at the gates, called out to the other men who were in ambush, and they all poured into the castle together, crowding by at the sides of the wagon. The wagon, being directly in the way, prevented the portcullis from being shut down. Thus the castle was taken.

Mr. George and Rollo also went to visit Melrose Abbey, which is a very beautiful ruin in the south part of Scotland. While they were there they visited Abbotsford, too, which is the house that Walter Scott lived in. Walter Scott amused

himself, during his lifetime, in collecting a great
many objects of interest connected with Scottish
history, and putting them up in his house; and
now the place is a perfect museum of Scottish
antiquities and curiosities.

Melrose and Abbotsford are in the southern
part of Scotland, not very far from the English
frontier. After visiting them, Mr. George and
Rollo proceeded by the railway to Berwick,
which stands on the boundary line; and there
they bade Scotland farewell.

www.ingramcontent.com/pod-product-compliance
Lightning Source LLC
Chambersburg PA
CBHW020319260626
47156CB00004B/1290